D0455216

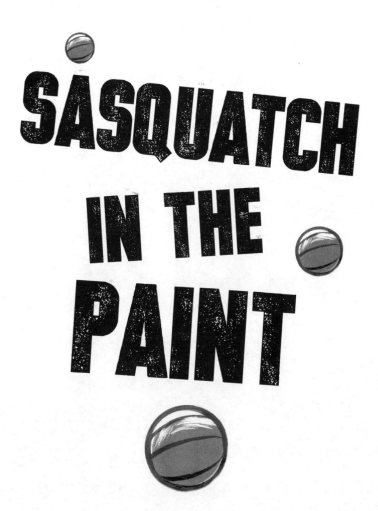

SASQUATCH IN THE PAINT

KAREEM ABDUL-JABBAR
AND RAYMOND OBSTFELD

SASQUATCH IN THE PAINT

Disney · HYPERION BOOKS

NEW YORK

First Edition
Printed in the United States of America
1 3 5 7 9 10 8 6 4 2

G475-5664-5-13196

Library of Congress Cataloging-in-Publication Data
Abdul-Jabbar, Kareem, 1947–
    Sasquatch in the paint/by Kareem Abdul-Jabbar and Raymond Obstfeld.—
First edition.
        pages cm.—(Streetball crew; book 1)
    Summary: Eighth-grader Theo Rollins' growth spurt has Coach Mandrake
trying to transform him into a basketball star, but training time is hurting
the science club's chances of winning the "Aca-lympics," and being accused of
stealing could mean Theo is off both teams.
    ISBN 978-1-4231-7870-5 (hardback)
    [1. Middle schools—Fiction. 2. Schools—Fiction. 3. Basketball—Fiction.
4. Science clubs—Fiction. 5. Interpersonal relations—Fiction. 6. African
Americans—Fiction. 7. Jews—United States—Fiction. 8. Mystery and
detective stories.] I. Obstfeld, Raymond, 1952 — II. Title.
    PZ7.A1589337Sas 2013
    [Fic]—dc23   2013007147

Reinforced binding

Visit www.disneyhyperionbooks.com

To my five children, who make me proud to be their dad.
—K. A-J.

For my home team, Harper and Max.
Life with you is the most fun and exciting game ever.
—R. O.

"HEY, Chewbacca! How do you say 'loser' in Wookie?"

Don't look, Theo told himself. Don't look! No good can come from looking.

He didn't look. Instead, he focused his attention on Danbury Heights' gum-chewing Number 8. The guard was dribbling the ball down court and holding up three fingers so his teammates knew which play to run. Number 8 looked so confident. Even the way he chewed his gum was confident, as if he was absolutely sure that the play would work and he was already seeing the two points up on the scoreboard.

Where did a thirteen-year-old get that kind of confidence? Theo wondered jealously. The only thing Theo felt confident about was . . . Nope, he couldn't think of anything.

"Looks like we finally found Bigfoot!" another Danbury Heights fan yelled. "Hey, Bigfoot, where ya been hiding all these years?"

A few kids liked that and started chanting, "Bigfoot! Bigfoot! Bigfoot!"

Don't look! Theo scolded himself again.

"Stop calling him Bigfoot!" a girl hollered. Grateful, Theo almost looked to see who his defender was. Until she laughed wickedly and said, "He prefers to be called by his proper name: Sasquatch!"

Theo could hear their harsh laughter as clearly as if he were sitting on the bleachers next to them.

But he wasn't on the bleachers, he was moving backward into the paint, keeping his arm bar pressed against the back of Danbury Heights' beefy center, Number 5, who clearly had eaten a spicy burrito before the game. He kept belching, and the smell reminded Theo of the outhouse he'd used at camp.

Mr. Mandrake, the Orangetree Middle School coach, had taught his players to keep an arm bar on the opponent's lower back. But Theo was five inches taller than the boy he was guarding. (In fact, he was taller than everyone else on the court, including the referees.) Unless he dropped to his knees, the lowest Theo could get his arm bar was on the kid's shoulder blades.

The game against Danbury Heights had just started twenty seconds ago and Theo was already sweating. Not from the exercise. So far all he'd done was move down the court. But the effort it took for him not to look over at the bleachers where his tormentors were whooping and yelling insults at him was exhausting. He'd rather run wind sprints. And wind sprints usually made him vomit.

Coach Mandrake had warned him this might happen.

"Theo, listen to me," he'd said, stroking his little hamster-like goatee as usual. Since that was the only hair on his entire head (except for his eyebrows), he seemed like he was always checking on it to make sure it was still there. "When those boys first see your height, they're going to be scared. And when kids are scared of something, they make fun of it. Don't let it get to you."

Here's what the coach meant:

Theo had grown six inches over the summer.

Six inches!

By August, he was taller than his dad, and his dad was a cop. When Theo had returned to school in the fall, he'd had to duck to enter the boys' bathroom. The urinal seemed so far away he felt like a long-distance sniper when using it. Most of the kids (and even the teachers) at school had been cool about his growth spurt, making dumb jokes about "the weather up there" and "have you seen Jack's beanstalk?" Lame stuff like that. A couple juniors from the high school had asked if he would buy beer for them. Some of his friends had tried to convince him to get them into an R-rated movie starring Seth Rogen and Jonah Hill. He'd said no to both and, thankfully, no one held it against him. It wasn't like Theo was suddenly popular, but he was getting noticed. A few students he didn't even know now nodded at him on the way to classes. Truthfully, after three years of invisibility at middle school, it felt kind of good.

"Bigfoot! Bigfoot! Bigfoot!" the chanting continued.

"Don't let him near the Empire State Building!" a boy shouted.

No one laughed. The chanting stopped.

"'Cuz he's King Kong!" the boy explained.

Then they laughed, though it sounded kind of forced. Theo figured that if they had to start explaining their jokes, maybe they were running out of giant things to compare him to. He started to make a mental list of what might come next: Statue of Liberty, Godzilla, Jolly Green Giant . . .

Focus on the game, he reminded himself.

He leaned into Number 5. Number 5 pushed back, moving him a few inches. Theo might have been taller, but Burrito Breath outweighed him by twenty pounds. When you distributed Theo's weight over six feet and four inches, you were left with a long, skinny stick figure of a kid. His legs had grown so suddenly that he felt a little wobbly on them, like he was walking on shaky stilts.

Number 8 chest-passed the ball to the bulky kid, who was growing a fuzzy mustache that looked like foot fungus. Fuzzy Mustache bounce-passed it to a short kid with spiked blond hair. Spiked Hair dribbled between his legs a few times, which caused the gang on the bleachers to yelp and whoop appreciation. Theo realized that most of the yelling was coming from the visitors' side. This was a home game, but hardly anyone from school was here. The only cheering on the home side came from a few scattered parents desperately trying to make up for the lack of supporters.

Theo suspected the bleachers were nearly empty because the basketball team was the worst sports team at Orangetree. The football team, the volleyball team, even the lacrosse team had huge trophies in the glass case near the school's entrance. But the basketball team had won nothing in the past four years. Most kids didn't even know the school *had* a basketball team. Theo hadn't known until Coach Mandrake had cornered him on the first day of school and said, "Boy, you did some serious growing over the summer. We're going to have to have us a talk."

They'd talked. And here he was. Panicky. Gawky. His throat so dry it scratched when he swallowed.

Spiked Hair passed the ball to Burrito Breath, Theo's guy. Theo stretched out his long arms and flapped them like bird wings. Up, down, to the left, to the right. Don't let him shoot, Theo chanted in his mind. Don't let the first points of the game be scored off you.

Burrito Breath dribbled left. Theo stayed with him. Burrito Breath dribbled right. Theo waved his arms, blocking any possible shot.

"Hey, freak, loved you in *Avatar!*" a bleacher kid yelled.

Don't look. Focus on the ball.

"But I preferred the *blue* skin!"

That got some oooooohhhs from the crowd, as if they were saying, "Oh no, he didn't go there." Theo was one of a dozen black kids in the school. There were a lot more Asians and Hispanics than African Americans. The color of his skin had never been an issue at school. Sometimes a kid would say something stupid, not even knowing he or she was being offensive, so Theo didn't take offense. But there had been a few times—in the city, among strangers—when he'd overheard remarks that definitely were meant to be racist.

Theo felt his skin burn. Don't look! Don'tlookdon'tlook don't . . .

He looked.

Saw their smirking faces.

That's all it took. . . .

Burrito Breath faked a pass to the left. Theo quickly slid over to block it. Burrito Breath spun to the right, leaped up, and tossed in an easy scoop shot.

The scoreboard flashed the two points in red.

Burrito Breath turned to Theo and said, "All day long, dude." Then he ran over and high-fived Number 8. Theo heard him laugh and say, "He's nothing. Just tall. No skills."

After that, things got even worse.

Yeah, you heard right.

"THANKS for losing us the game, *Bigfoot*," Roger McDonald snarled as the Ravens filed out of the gym toward the locker room. He angrily smacked the metal water fountain as he passed it.

"You blew it, Rollins," Sinjin James agreed. He smacked the water fountain, too. Clearly, they wished that the fountain were Theo's head.

Theo didn't say anything. Roger and Sinjin weren't wrong.

No one else said anything. Theo couldn't decide which was worse, Roger's and Sinjin's angry insults or knowing the rest of the players were all thinking the same thing.

"Team meeting," Coach Mandrake announced, hurrying past the boys into the locker room. "Right now. Let's go, boys. Hustle, hustle, hustle."

Great, Theo thought. Team meeting. More insults. More humiliation.

Theo looked over his shoulder back into the gym. He was at least a head taller than the rest of the team, so his gaze skimmed over the tops of their shiny, sweaty heads.

The Danbury Heights players were high-fiving, hugging their parents, and laughing at something their coach was saying. Theo's teammates marched with heads hung down like handcuffed convicts shuffling back from the sunny exercise yard into their dark cells.

He saw Burrito Breath pointing at him, then whispering to his pal, Number 8. They both laughed. Burrito Breath laughed so hard he started coughing.

Behind them, up in the bleachers, Theo saw the girl who'd called him Sasquatch. She was eating a red Twizzler. She said something to the two guys beside her and they laughed.

Everyone seemed to be laughing.

Everyone except Theo.

And his team.

And Coach Mandrake.

In the locker room, Coach stood while the ten boys on the team took seats on the wooden benches. The overhead lights glistened off his bald head. He stroked his goatee while he waited for everyone's attention.

"First," he said cheerfully, "I want to congratulate you boys on a game well played."

Roger snorted and looked down at the ground.

Coach frowned at Roger. "You got something to say, Roger? Let's hear it?"

Roger shook his head, his eyes still on the ground.

Coach Mandrake continued: "Now, I know today's outcome is not the one we'd all hoped for, but it's only the first game of the season. We've got plenty more ahead of us."

Weston Zheng, the team comedian, piped up, "At least no one comes to the games, so the rest of the school won't even know we lost."

A couple guys chuckled.

Roger scowled at Weston. "Maybe if we start winning, they'll start coming."

"Yeah, Coach," Sinjin agreed. "I'm tired of being a school joke."

Most the boys started chattering at that. Lots of "yeah"s and "that would be awesome"s and a stray "fat chance." Someone said "deadweight" and a couple kids looked at Theo.

Only Theo and Chris Richards remained silent. Chris was the team's best player, but he didn't talk much. The only time he spoke was to call out plays. During the weeks of practice before today, he'd never made fun of Theo like most the others, but he hadn't offered any encouragement either. All the other guys respected him because he was so good and because he was generous at passing off the ball so they could shoot.

"I agree," Coach Mandrake said. "This is the year we turn things around. We make a name for this team. Fill those bleachers with butts and fill that trophy case with trophies. Then everyone will know our team and they'll know your names!"

Theo could feel a glimmer of hope rising among the other boys. They sat up straighter. Allowed themselves a smile. Roger and Sinjin fist-bumped.

"So, toward that end, we're going to make some major changes," Coach said. He pointed at Theo.

Here it comes, Theo thought. I'm off the team. One-Game Wonder. Except I wasn't a wonder, more like a blunder.

"I've decided we're going to build our entire offense around Theo."

The coach's statement dropped on the players like a bomb. Everyone turned to look at Theo as if they were surprised he was still sitting there. As if his body should have just vaporized in shame.

"What?" Roger hollered. "But, Coach, he sucks!"

Ordinarily, Coach wouldn't have allowed anyone to rag on a teammate like that. Laps or push-ups or wind sprints would have been the punishment. But this time, he ignored the taunt. Instead, he rubbed his hands enthusiastically like he was a criminal mastermind hatching a brilliant scheme. "Boys, take the weekend to practice your shooting. On Monday we come back with a whole new attitude and a whole new game plan. The rest of the season will rest on Theo's very tall shoulders." He smiled at Theo as if Theo should be grateful for this vote of confidence.

What Coach didn't see were the nine other sweaty faces staring at him as if they'd just found the guy who'd invented homework.

"PERHAPS no one told you, Theo, but Fridays are supposed to be fun," Brian "Brainiac" Horowitz said. "Last day of school. Chillin' for the weekend. No more teachers' dirty looks and cafeteria's disgusting food. Mondays are for humiliation and nausea, not Fridays."

Theo didn't say anything. Just stared at the ground.

"But you've twisted that all around. Now that you're a jock, you've turned easygoing Fridays into horrifying Mondays." In a terrible English accent: "May I have another helping of embarrassment, sir?"

"I made a big mistake," Theo said. "A huge mistake."

"No duh," Brian agreed. "You looked like a cocker spaniel in those dog-food commercials. You know, where he's running on wood floors trying to get to the food, but it's so slippery that his legs keep sliding out from under him. Except you're not as cute."

Theo didn't respond. He was busy replaying the entire game in his head. For the hundredth time. "I let those punks from Danbury Heights get to me. That skin-color comment shook me."

Brian snorted. "Yeah, that's the reason you sucked."

Theo frowned at his friend's sarcasm. "You wouldn't understand."

"Right. Because I'm white. There's no way a chubby white Jew with thick glasses, a wild Jew-fro, and perpetual acne could understand the emotional effects of name-calling. Thank goodness my life has been so full of unicorns and rainbows."

Theo grinned. "Then you agree."

Brian punched Theo in the arm. "As McLandburgh Wilson said, 'The optimist sees the donut, the pessimist sees the hole.'"

That's how Brian always talked, like he was a teacher. A really sarcastic teacher. He couldn't help it; he was just very smart. For a while he'd tried forcing himself to sound like all the other kids by using a lot of slang ("Yo, my dudes. What up wid dat Monet?"). The problem was that he got all his slang phrases by researching online, which meant that some of them hadn't yet made their way to Orangetree Middle School, so he had to explain what he was saying. ("A Monet," he clarified patiently, "is someone who looks good from a distance, but up close looks like a mess. Like Monet's paintings." To which the kid responded, "Who's Monet?") Naturally, that experiment didn't last long. He returned to nerdspeak, which most people found just as hard to understand. But Theo liked that about him.

Theo and Brian sat on the swings in the little kids'

playground section of Palisades Park. It was close to dinnertime, so the place was empty except for one giggling toddler stumbling around the padded pirate ship while his mom cheered him on. Theo looked at the mom's delighted face and felt a pain in his stomach. Tears threatened to leak out. He blinked hard and turned away. No need to go there, he scolded himself, forcing himself not to picture his own mom's face. He already felt bad enough.

"Isn't your dad expecting you?" Brian asked, looking at his watch.

"I told him I would probably hang out with the team after the game."

Brian didn't say anything. No need. After the team meeting, the other players had gathered their gear and left. No one asked Theo to hang out or go for pizza or a Jamba Juice. No one even spoke to him. They were all too stunned by Coach Mandrake's announcement.

"Why did they name this Palisades Park?" Brian said. "A palisade is a fence that forms a barrier. Or it's a line of cliffs. You see any fences or cliffs around here?"

"Your mom sometimes calls you her 'handsome boy.' You see any handsomeness on that ugly mug?"

"So, it's like when you slapped hands with the other team and they said, 'Good game'?"

Theo punched Brian in the arm. Brian punched Theo back. They exchanged a few more punches, each one harder than the last.

"Dude, that hurt," Brian winced, rubbing his arm.

"At least you have some flesh to protect your bone," Theo said, rubbing his own sore arm.

"Great. A fat joke. From a stork."

Theo punched him again and they both laughed.

The swings were too small for them. Too small for Brian because he was just as chubby as he'd described himself and the chains cut painfully into his wide butt. Too small for Theo because his long legs had to stick straight out like planks of wood. Both boys were uncomfortable, yet they didn't move. They'd been playing at this park since they were both six, though they'd stopped coming a couple years ago. The park seemed so confining compared with the vast borderless empires on the Internet.

"What are we doing here anyway?" Brian asked. "Traditionally, feeling sorry for yourself is accompanied by mass quantities of sweets, preferably the frozen kind. Whipped cream and cherries are often involved."

"I thought you were on a diet," Theo said.

"Hey, when my best friend is hurting, I'm willing to make sacrifices."

Theo laughed. "Gee, thanks, friend."

"I'm not your friend, buddy."

"I'm not your buddy, pal."

"I'm not your pal, guy."

They both laughed. Even though they'd done this routine from *South Park* a million times, it never got old. The edgy animated show was one of their favorites, but they'd learned to be careful about who was around when they talked about it. If it was just their friends, that was okay, because all the kids at school joked about episodes from *South Park* and *Family Guy*. But if an adult, especially a parent, was around, there'd be eye rolling, disappointed head shaking, and sometimes a boring lesson on good citizenship.

Once, Theo's dad had overheard them laughing about the "Night of the Living Homeless" episode of *South Park*. In the episode, the bad economy causes the number of homeless people in South Park to increase. Everyone treats them like diseased zombies, because their touch can make others homeless, too. Mr. Rollins had immediately launched into a loud lecture about the plight of the homeless and how a lot of people in their neighborhood were just one paycheck away from living in their cars.

"It's just a TV show, Dad," Theo had said.

"I know it's a TV show, T," his dad had replied. "I also know that the show isn't making fun of the homeless, it's making fun of the people that have no compassion for those going through hard times. I want to make sure you understand that important difference."

"Yes, Dad, I get it," Theo had said with big sigh. In truth, though, he hadn't really thought about it one way or the other. He'd just thought the show was funny. Period.

Why did everything have to be such a big deal with his dad lately? Every conversation turned into a training video for good citizenship. It felt like his dad was always watching him for signs that he was going to do something evil. Maybe that's how all dads acted. Or maybe it was because Theo's mom had been dead for over a year and he was worried that his fatherly influence wasn't enough to keep Theo from turning into some sort of low-pants-wearing, underwear-showing gangsta.

"Are we getting ice cream or what?" Brian asked, struggling to wriggle out of the swing. Once free, he adjusted his pants. "This thing gave me a worse wedgie than Billy Adams did in the third grade. Remember him?"

"Sure. Wet Willy Billy. He liked to give everyone wet willies. Wedgies were just a sideline."

Brian laughed. "Yeah, I forgot about that."

Theo stood up, towering over Brian. It was weird being this much taller than his friend. It was only eight inches, the length of a banana, but the distance felt much greater, like he was looking at Brian through the wrong end of a telescope. Almost like they were living in two different worlds. He wondered if Brian felt the same way. He also wondered why he didn't say anything about how he felt to Brian. Before the summer, he'd shared everything with him. Especially his feelings about his mother; outside of his father, Brian was the only one he trusted with those.

But things were different now. He couldn't explain why.

Was it just the height? The length of a banana? Or was he going through something he didn't think even Brian would understand? Like he was not just growing tall, but he was also growing away from everybody and everything.

"I'm not getting ice cream," Theo said. "That's not why we're here."

Brian looked over at the snack stand in the nearby building. In the window, a cotton-candy machine puffed pink swirls. He sighed. "Then why are we here? To torture me?"

"I'm going over there." Theo pointed at the three full basketball courts. One court was usually set aside for middle schoolers, one for high schoolers, and the third for all the dads with knee braces and smelly ointments and other older guys with jobs. The third group usually came later, after dinner with their families. The courts were lit, so people played until the park closed at eleven.

It was still early enough that only two half-court games were going on. The players moved lazily, as if just waiting for more players to show up before they turned up their game.

Brian laughed, as if Theo had told a joke. "Why would you go down there? Are you running low on your daily quota of humiliation? Seriously, dude, that tank is full."

"I need to practice. I can't play another game like today. I just can't." Theo didn't tell Brian about Coach's new plan. Or the ginormous amount of pressure he felt. He couldn't go back to school on Monday and be as terrible as he was today.

Brian sighed. "Is it possible—and I'm only spitballing here—that you simply aren't a very good basketball player? Just because you're tall doesn't mean you're automatically a basketball phenom. Just because I'm a nerdy Jew doesn't mean I'm destined to study law or medicine. Actually, I really do want to be a lawyer, so, bad example. But you know what I mean."

Theo started walking toward the courts. "I have to try, dude. I can't explain it."

"It seems like lately there's a lot going on with you that you can't explain." There was an edge in Brian's voice. Theo hadn't been sure whether or not Brian had noticed Theo holding back lately. Now he knew.

"Yeah, I know," Theo said quietly. "I wish there wasn't."

Brian's expression softened. "I'm not going with you. That's a wedgie minefield down there. One wrong step and bam!" He made a yanking motion as if hoisting a pair of underpants. "Casualties could be severe."

"I'll protect you, Cowardly Lion. Since I grew, no one wants to mess with me."

"Yeah, right. One punch and you'd fold like wet toilet paper."

"Probably. But they don't know that." Theo grinned and nodded for Brian to follow him.

Brian didn't move. "What about studying for the Brain Train? We face Lansing in a couple weeks and you're our science expert."

The Brain Train was the name of Orangetree's Aca-lympics team, a group of academically gifted students who competed against other middle school nerds in a game-show format that tested knowledge in a variety of school-related subjects. Last year, Theo and Brian had been alternates because they were only in seventh grade. This year, they were in eighth grade and made up two of the five-member first team.

"I'll be ready," Theo said. "Go ahead, test me."

Brian took out his phone and clicked to a page of science questions. "How many bones in the human body?"

"Trick question. In adults there are two hundred and six. But children have three hundred until a few of them fuse together as they grow."

"What's the smallest bone in the body?"

"The stirrup bone in the middle ear. It's point-eleven inches long. Okay, can I go now?"

Brian held up his hand like a traffic cop. "Where are the ears on a cricket?"

"On the front legs, just below the knees. Right?"

"How should I know? I just wrote down the questions, not the answers."

Theo started down the slope toward the courts. "See ya later."

"Come on, Theo. Let's go celebrate Friday like nature intended. With artificially sweetened treats!"

Theo waved as he continued on. "I'll call you."

"Don't bother. Just directly dial 911 for the ambulance."

Theo laughed to show Brian he knew what he was doing. But as he got closer to the basketball courts, he felt his stomach tighten. Maybe this wasn't such a good idea after all.

His aching stomach's warning was confirmed when he saw a girl his age shooting free throws by herself on the adult court. She sank five in a row before noticing him. She stopped, shaded her eyes for a better look, and then marched straight toward him. He recognized her as the girl from the bleachers.

The one who'd called him Sasquatch.

"MAN, you sure stank up the court today," she said. She dribbled the ball as she talked. It distracted Theo, like someone snapping fingers in his face.

He tried to pass her as if she wasn't there.

She slid in front of him. "Major fail, dude. Was that your first time playing?"

His heart thumped with anger. She talked so casually, like they were friends instead of mortal enemies. It was as if the Joker came up to Batman and said, "Wanna grab a movie, Bats?"

Theo wanted to say something really mean, call her some nasty names, see how she liked it. He looked at her, searching for a target he could mock. Maybe something about her short haircut ("You look like a boy!") or freckled nose and cheeks ("Somebody shoot you in the face with a paintball?"). But he decided to just ignore her, be the mature one.

He kept walking.

"Rude much?" she snorted.

Theo spun and barked, "Me? I'm the rude one? You

and your pals heckled me the whole game! You called me Sasquatch!"

So much for being the mature one.

She chuckled. "Yeah. That was pretty funny."

"Funny? How was it funny? It was hurtful."

"Boo-hoo. If you're gonna cry, call the wambulance. I'm a girl, dude. A girl with short hair who plays basketball, whose family is—" She broke off abruptly. "You wanna hear some of the names I get called?"

Theo didn't say anything. Actually, he was a little embarrassed to think of some of the names he'd called girls when hanging with his guy friends. At least he'd never done it to their faces.

She stopped dribbling and pinned the ball against her hip. She looked him over and frowned. "You aren't going to blame me for how badly you played, are you? Because you looked like someone learning to ice-skate for the first time." She dropped the ball and did an imitation of someone trying to keep his balance on the ice. She laughed, which sounded like someone shaking a can full of nickels.

"Whatever," Theo said, and started walking away again.

"'Whatever?' I see you're just as good with words as you are with a basketball."

Theo kept walking, grinding his teeth in anger.

She grabbed her basketball and caught up to him, dribbling as they walked. "Anyway, they weren't my friends. I just happened to be sitting next to them."

"And because they were yelling stuff, you had to, too?"

She shrugged. "I didn't have to. But it made the game more fun. To be honest, both teams kinda sucked. Yours happened to suck more."

Theo stopped walking and looked at her. She had reddish-brown hair cut in a bowl shape, a massive spray of freckles across her nose and cheeks, and an expression on her face that said she wouldn't take crap from anyone. Mess with her, that expression said, and expect to get it back—twice as bad. She was athletic-looking and wore blue basketball shorts that hung below her knees and a red Philadelphia 76ers jersey with the number 6 on it.

She saw Theo looking at her jersey. "Dr. J's number," she said proudly.

Theo shrugged. He'd heard of Dr. J, but he had no idea who exactly he was or why he was called "doctor." He'd never followed sports of any kind. That was his dad's thing.

She wrinkled her nose at his apparent indifference. "You don't even know who Dr. J is, do you? Julius Erving. Fifth top scorer in NBA history. He got his nickname in high school from a friend. Julius called his friend 'professor' and his friend called him 'doctor.' It stuck. Later, when he became so good at the slam dunk, they called him the Doctor of Dunk. Cool, huh?"

Theo shrugged again.

She shook her head in disgust. "No wonder you stink at basketball. You've got no appreciation for the game or its history."

Theo leaned down so his face was close to hers and glared. "Yeah? Do you know who Magnus Carlsen, Levon Aronian, and Vladimir Kramnik are?"

She seemed to lift up on her toes to return his glare. When she didn't answer, Theo straightened up and grinned. "See? The world doesn't revolve around basketball. There are other things. More important things."

She put the basketball on her finger and spun it like a globe. "Those are the three top-ranked chess players in the world. Carlsen from Norway, Aronian from Armenia, and Kramnik from Russia."

Theo's jaw dropped open like a cartoon animal's. He was surprised it didn't clunk against the ground.

She laughed. "Lookin' smart there, Sasquatch. Hey, maybe because of me, your nickname will be 'Sasquatch.' When you're famous they'll mention me in the Wikipedia entry about you. 'Cute, awesome girl he knew who used to beat his butt at basketball.' How's that sound?"

"You haven't beat me at anything."

She nodded toward the court. "You wanna try me, Sasquatch?"

"Shut up," Theo snapped.

"Wow, nice comeback. Didn't your mom ever teach you not to say 'shut up'?"

"My mom's dead." Theo hadn't meant to say that. There was something about her that made him just blurt things out. She'd make a good cop.

She shrugged as if his mom dying was no big deal, as

if he'd told her he'd stubbed his toe. "So, what happened?" she asked. "You go through some growth spurt over the summer and they dragged you onto the team? You're some kind of nerd and you saw this as a chance to have everyone see you differently? Win the big game, get the hot cheerleader?"

Theo sighed. There was no point in faking it with this girl. "Pretty much."

"Now you know, height's not the main thing in round-ball. What you need is some sort of *Karate Kid*–Miyagi guru who'll lay down all that wax-on-wax-off stuff. Only about basketball."

"I suppose that would be you," Theo said with a snort.

She laughed. "Me? No way, dude. I don't have the patience. And the poor dope who teaches you is going to need a lot of patience. But I know someone who might help."

"For a fee?" Theo said smugly.

"That's between you and him."

A scam. He should have guessed.

"No thanks. I already got a coach."

She shrugged. "Suit yourself."

Just then, a motorcycle revved loudly nearby. Her head jerked up at the sound. Theo noticed a shift in her expression. Not scared exactly, but something close. Like someone bracing to take a charge from a much bigger player.

The biker was parked on the jogging path, which had

signs forbidding skates, skateboards, and bicycles. He was dressed all in black leather and wore a shiny black helmet with red flames on the side and a dark visor.

Theo couldn't see his face, but he seemed to be looking straight at the girl.

"Do you know him?" Theo asked.

But she was already walking up the slope to meet Motorcycle Guy. He whipped off his helmet. He looked like he was about eighteen, with crow-black hair and dark skin. Not as dark as Theo's, but definitely surfer tan.

The biker immediately started talking to her in a foreign language Theo didn't understand. It seemed kind of Russian, the way he sounded like he was chewing tough meat while talking.

She answered in English with, "I don't care."

The reply seemed to anger the biker even more. He stomped on the kickstand so the bike wouldn't fall, and jumped off with an athletic grace that Theo admired. He marched up to the girl, grabbed her by the shoulders, and hollered in her face, "This is your last chance!"

She shook her head and hollered back, "Leave me alone!"

He shouted something in that foreign language.

She jerked free from his grip and said, "Mind your own business."

He slapped her across the face so hard she fell to the ground. Her basketball slipped from under her arm and rolled away. Theo wasn't sure what shocked him more, the sudden slap, or the fact that she went down. He'd imagined her too tough to be knocked down by anything less than a truck.

The girl—Theo realized that he didn't know her name—stood up, rubbed her face where she'd been smacked, and kicked Motorcycle Guy hard in the shin. He groaned at the contact and hobbled back a few steps from the pain. He shouted some words in that foreign language and raised his hand high as if to slap her again, harder.

"Hey!" Theo heard himself shout. Then he realized his feet were running up the slope toward Motorcycle Guy. He didn't remember telling his feet to do that. In fact, he wasn't at all happy about the direction they were heading. Because there was no way he could beat up Motorcycle Guy. Yet he was still running up that slope, still yelling things like "Leave her alone!" and holding up his cell phone: "I've already called 911!" Actually, that would have been a good idea. He started to press the numbers when Motorcycle Guy turned his head and looked at him. He stared as if memorizing Theo's face, which made Theo's stomach drop.

Then Motorcycle Guy jammed his helmet back onto his head, limped to his bike, climbed on, and roared off.

"You okay?" Theo said, a little breathless after running up the slope.

There were no tears in her eyes. She didn't shout angrily

after him. She just stood without any expression at all. "Of course," she said, as if that was a silly question. "You just have to roll with the punch. Didn't anyone ever teach you how to fight?"

"I've never been in a fight."

She frowned at that, as if unsure whether he was lying or crazy. Then she shrugged and said, "Probably just as well, because you're not in very good shape. I thought you'd pass out running up this slope."

"You're welcome," Theo said. He picked up her basketball and handed it to her. "Who was that guy? What language was that? Why did he hit you?"

She smiled at him, the side of her face bright red from the slap. Then suddenly she ran off, calling over her shoulder, "See you around, Sasquatch."

"HEY, Stretch! You wanna play? We need a sixth man."

Theo looked down at the five boys standing on the basketball court. They'd been shooting around since he'd arrived, waiting for another player to show up. Theo wondered if they'd seen Motorcycle Guy slap the girl. If they had, why hadn't they joined him in running over to help her?

Help her? Is that what he'd done?

Now that Theo thought about it, what actual help had he been? He was tall, sure, but he couldn't fight. One slap from Motorcycle Guy and he'd have floated away like a kite. Theo saw himself more as a scarecrow. Trying to look fierce and scary, but powerless to stop the crows from eating the crops if they really wanted to. That seemed to be his role on the basketball court, too.

Maybe that should be his nickname: "Scarecrow."

Theo glanced over his shoulder to where Crazy Girl had gone. Crazy Girl. Yeah, that should be her nickname. She didn't make any sense.

No sign of her. What had Motorcycle Guy wanted from

her? What would he do the next time he caught up with her? Or Theo?

Theo shook off the questions. Not his problem. After all, she'd been the one to run off. And she'd called him Sasquatch during the game. She'd led the chanting. He didn't owe her anything.

Theo joined the other boys on the court. They were all older than him by a year or two. He recognized two ninth graders from Valley Crest High School. They didn't seem to recognize him. Why would they? He'd been pretty invisible last year.

He was one of fourteen black kids at a school of six hundred. You'd think that would have made him stand out more, but it had just the opposite effect. To many of the students, he was just "one of the black kids." He didn't blame them. The school had about three hundred Asian kids and a hundred Hispanic kids and sometimes he thought of them as "one of the Asians" or "one of the Hispanics." Brian said there were about thirty Jewish kids, but Theo only knew of Brian and Isaac (who wore one of those little Jewish beanies). When Theo asked who the others were, Brian said he wouldn't out the others, because they were trying to go through school undercover, like spies. If no one knew who they were, no one could pick on them.

"I'm not that good," Theo warned the kids on the court. Better to lower their expectations right away, he figured. No slam dunks or alley-oops today, boys.

"Don't worry about it," the Asian kid said. He grinned

a little, as if he thought Theo was just pretending not to be good. Sandbagging. He tossed the basketball to Theo. "You wanna take a few shots to warm up?"

Theo nodded. One of the boys pulled off his shirt and jogged over to the water fountain for a drink. The other four waited for Theo to take his warm-up shots. Theo stared at the basket as if it were a giant dragon waiting to swallow him whole. Throwing a ball at it would only make it mad. His stomach tightened again and his skin felt cold. He was glad Crazy Girl wasn't around to see this.

"You guys see that kid on the motorcycle?" Theo asked, stalling.

They shrugged, which Theo took to mean yes.

"Did you see him hit that girl?"

"No," one of them said. He didn't sound convincing.

"You know who that guy was?" Theo pressed.

The boys looked at one another, then at Theo. Asian Kid said, "You gonna shoot or what?"

They didn't seem to care about what happened, as if it had taken place in another country or in a movie instead of fifty yards up a grassy slope. Or maybe they were scared of Motorcycle Guy, too.

Theo took some practice shots from the free throw line. Half of them went in, which was better than he'd expected, especially with five boys watching him. He wasn't a bad shot as long as he wasn't moving. And no one was guarding him. And his legs weren't shaking.

"Let's play," said the kid with the reddest hair Theo had

ever seen. Red grabbed the ball from Theo and walked out to the three-point line. "You're with us. What's your name?"

Theo told him. Then everyone gave their names, but Theo was so nervous that he immediately forgot all of them.

"Clear all possessions back to the three," Red explained quickly, anxious to get the game going. "Points are ones and twos."

"Ones and twos?" Theo asked.

Theo heard one of the kids sigh, the way you sigh when you're trying to explain something to a younger child and he's not getting it. *This is the way you tie a shoelace: the rabbit ears go . . .*

"Anything past the three-point line is worth two points. Everything else is worth one."

"Right," Theo said. "Of course. Ones and twos."

Red stared at him, obviously waiting for Theo to do something. Theo didn't know what, so he just stood still.

"We're on offense," Red said.

Theo thought: Offense means we have the ball; defense means they have the ball. He nodded and moved to the three-point line. Asian Kid guarded him. Shirtless was also on Theo's team. Shirtless started cutting toward the basket.

Red threw Theo the ball. Theo dribbled a couple times, then threw it to Red, relieved to be rid of it. It was like holding a ticking bomb covered in dog poop.

"Go under!" Red shouted. He waved for Theo to force Asian Kid into the key so they could lob the ball to him for an easy turnaround layup. With his height advantage, there was no way Asian Kid could block him. That was pretty much the same play Coach Mandrake had worked on with Theo. "Use your reach, Theo," the coach had said.

Theo pushed his butt out and backed toward the basket. Asian Kid pushed back, but he was too thin to stop Theo. Red raised the ball over his head and motioned as if to toss it to Theo. As soon as he did, the kid guarding Red reversed a few steps to help double-team Theo. That left Red wide open, so he took the jumper from the free throw line.

He missed.

The ball bounced off the rim and dropped to the ground near Theo. He reached for it, but Asian Kid zipped around him, grabbed the ball, dribbled out to the three-point line, and then came back straight in for a layup. Theo managed to slide close enough to reach one hand out and block the shot. He couldn't believe he'd actually done that. When Asian Kid landed on the ground, he was off balance enough that Theo could grab the ball right out of his hands. He turned and immediately shot it from one foot away. The ball banked off the backboard and dropped through the net.

Inside, Theo was throwing a Super Bowl party. Streamers. Balloons. Cheerleaders. Nine-layer dip with those scoop chips he loved. His dad was high-fiving him—

"Dude, you have to clear the ball," Shirtless said, annoyed.

"What?" Theo said.

"Clear all changes of possession. That means that if the ball goes from one team to the other, you have to dribble the ball back to the three-point line before you can shoot again."

"Didn't you see me do that?" Asian Kid asked.

"Where you from?" Red asked, with a pinched expression that indicated he expected the answer to be somewhere beyond Mars.

"No basket," Asian Kid said a little too smugly. He tossed the ball to Red.

"Zero to zero," Red said. He chest-passed the ball to Shirtless, who did some fancy dribbling before tossing in a smooth eight-footer.

"One to nothing," Red said from the top of the key.

The game was only to eleven points, but it seemed to take forever. Theo did manage to score a basket, but Red and Shirtless made the rest of their points. Anytime they lobbed the ball to Theo, Asian Kid would hack at his arms until Theo panicked and passed the ball back out to Red or Shirtless. Theo's arms were sore from being smacked, and the backs of his hands were bleeding from Asian Kid's fingernails. During one play, Asian Kid smacked him so hard that it sounded like the loud slap Motorcycle Guy had given the girl. Everyone had stopped playing at the sound.

"C'mon, Jeremy," Red scolded Asian Kid, who shrugged. Then Red turned to Theo with even more disgust on his face. "Dude, you gotta call those fouls."

"Okay," Theo said, his voice so low he could barely hear it himself. He didn't want to tell them that he wasn't exactly sure what a foul was. He knew you couldn't hit or push the other player, but the line between aggressive play and fouling was blurry.

"Game point," Shirtless said, tossing the ball to Red.

They needed one point to win. One lousy basket. Theo really wanted that last basket to come from him, to prove himself to these guys. He didn't know why that was so important. They weren't especially nice to him. Once they realized he'd been telling the truth when he'd said he wasn't very good at basketball, they barely tolerated him. He noticed them constantly looking off the court, as if hoping for new players to show up to take his place. Even if he made the basket, their opinion of him probably wouldn't change. He'd already made too many dumb mistakes.

Still, he had to try.

He had to at least prove to himself that whatever Coach's plan was for him on Monday, he wouldn't make a complete idiot out of himself.

Theo raised his arm like a periscope above the others' heads. "Here," he said, calling for the ball. Red glanced up from his between-the-legs dribbling exhibition long enough to see Theo's hand waving for the ball. Red looked skeptical and tried to drive toward the basket himself. But his defender slid right along with him, swatting at the ball like an octopus on Red Bull. After a couple more failed attempts to dribble around his defender, Red looked over at Shirtless. The boy defending Shirtless was in position to intercept any pass. Finally, looking like someone about to flush his allowance down a toilet, Red lobbed the ball to Theo.

Theo caught it. (Okay, that was the easy part, he reminded himself.) Next he brought the ball down to his chest like Coach had shown him. He felt Asian Kid's forearm pushing hard against his lower back, trying to keep him off balance. The kid's bony forearm felt like a baseball bat grinding against his spine. Theo clenched his entire body and took a step backward, moving Asian Kid backward, too. He was surprised that he was able to do it. Then, suddenly, Theo spun hard to his left, jumped up, and laid the ball against the backboard. It dropped through the hoop with barely a sound against the net. Like a sigh of relief.

Yes! Theo screamed in his head.

Yesyesyesyesyes!

He won the game!

He turned to look at his teammates for some celebration, some whoops of appreciation. A "Nice shot" or "Good job." But they were all glaring angrily at him. Except for Asian Kid, who was lying on the ground with globs of blood dripping from his nose.

Asian Kid shouted some nasty R-rated curses at Theo.

Red shook his head in disgust at Theo. "Not cool, dude."

"Watch those elbows, man," Shirtless warned.

Elbows? Theo hadn't felt anything when he'd spun around.

Horrified, he ran to Asian Kid. "I'm sorry, man. I didn't realize . . ." He didn't know what else to say, so he offered his hand to help him up.

Asian Kid didn't take it. Instead, he wiped the back of his hand across his nose. Seeing the smear of bright red blood seemed to make him even angrier. Suddenly he jumped up and swung a fist into Theo's face.

Theo saw the fist coming in time to tilt his head back slightly. The punch glanced off his cheek. "Glance" in the same way that a hammer might "glance" off a nail. Meaning: it still hurt! A lot.

Theo rocked backward, stumbling a few steps. His cheek burned and ached at the same time. This was the first time he'd ever been hit in the face. In fourth grade he'd gotten into a fight at recess with Kevin Dubinsky over whose turn it was with the tetherball. But that had been more of a shoving match than a fight. Two shoves from each and the bell rang and that was the end of the fight. The next day they were back playing handball together.

But this was a real fight.

Real blood.

Real pain.

Real fear.

Theo wanted to run away. When he was shorter (was that really only three months ago?), he might have gotten away with running. These kids were older, so they probably would have expected it. But he was big now, bigger than they were. He hadn't thought about that before, about how being taller made people think of you as older, and they'd expect you to act older, too. He hadn't just grown; in everyone's eyes, he'd also aged a few years.

So running was out. He balled his fingers into fists, brought them up to his chest, and waited to see what Asian Kid would do next. His legs shook and he fought the panic rising in his gut.

Asian Kid cocked his fist back as if to take another swing. Theo lifted his skinny arms up to protect his face.

Then Shirtless stepped behind Asian Kid and pinned his arms to his sides. "Okay, Jeremy, that's enough. He didn't mean it."

Asian Kid—Jeremy—struggled against his friend's grip, but not that hard. He seemed content to let it go.

Theo dropped his fists. "I'm really sorry, Jeremy. It was an accident."

Jeremy responded with another string of curses.

Theo walked away, his cheek throbbing. Gingerly, he touched the sore spot and felt a golf-ball-size bump growing beneath his fingers.

He sighed. At least his day couldn't get any worse, he thought.

As usual, he was wrong.

THEO'S dad's gun was sitting on the kitchen table when Theo got home.

It lay on some paper towels between the butter dish and the pepper grinder like a coiled rattlesnake. It glistened from freshly applied oil. Theo rarely saw the gun, but whenever he did it gave him both a chill of excitement on the back of his neck and a burning dread in his stomach. The excitement was because it was the thing that protected his dad, though his dad had never drawn his gun in the line of duty in his fourteen years as a cop. The bad thing was that the gun reminded Theo that his dad's job was dangerous. When you had only one parent, you didn't want to be reminded of that. You really didn't.

Theo's dad came into the kitchen then. "Sorry, T," his dad said, grabbing the gun from the table. "I just finished cleaning it." He hurried off to his bedroom to lock it in the gun safe. He was in such a hurry he hadn't yet gotten a look at the damage to Theo's face.

Other kids thought it was so cool to have a cop for a dad, because they figured his dad could pretty much do anything he wanted. True, his dad was big and muscular and carried a badge and a gun. But he was also gentle and soft-spoken. And he never used the fact that he was a cop to get anything. Sometimes people tried to give him free stuff, but he wouldn't take it. Not even an ice-cream cone! He insisted on paying for everything—even the speeding ticket he'd gotten during a family vacation in Santa Barbara. Theo thought he'd get out of the ticket by showing the motorcycle cop his badge. But he didn't. He just took the ticket, said, "Thank you, Officer," and drove off.

"Why didn't you show him your badge, Dad?" Theo had asked him.

"Because I was speeding," his dad had said.

"But you could have gotten out of it," Theo persisted. "Saved some money."

Then Theo's mom turned around with a smile and said, "Your dad would rather do the right thing than the easy thing."

Theo had snorted, thinking, Another parental pearl of wisdom about Doing the Right Thing.

That year, it seemed like no matter what happened (a dirty cereal bowl, a misplaced iPod, an empty toilet roll), his mom would turn it into a Do the Right Thing lesson. But that day, when Theo saw the way his mom slid her arm around his dad's shoulder and the way his dad looked over at her, he kind of got it. Getting that bright beaming smile from Mom was worth doing extra chores, working harder on schoolwork, and, he guessed, paying speeding tickets.

Theo sat heavily at the table as he once again realized there was nothing he could ever do for the rest of his life to see that smile again. To have her hold his face in her hands, her eyes filling with tears, and say, "You make me so proud, sweetheart."

"Mom," he said aloud, surprising himself. He did that sometimes when he really, *really* missed her.

What would she think of him now, sitting here with a bruised cheek from fighting? After giving another kid a bloody nose? Sure, it was an accident, but if he hadn't been so anxious to show those kids what he could do, he might have been more careful. What would she have thought if she'd watched him play at school today, missing shots, letting his guy score, throwing passes that got intercepted? He'd even dribbled on his own foot, sending the ball skidding out of bounds. Someone from the stands had yelled that his nickname should be "Turnovers."

"What the heck happened to your face?" his dad said. He stood in front of Theo with a frilly red kitchen apron over his blue police uniform. Any other time, Theo might have laughed and made a joke about it.

"Basketball," Theo said, hoping that would end it. He didn't want to have to explain that he got into a fight.

His dad stared at him a few seconds, then turned, opened the freezer door, and pulled out a bag of corn. "Put this on it. It'll bring the swelling down."

Theo eased it onto the bruise. The cold instantly numbed the pain.

His dad yanked some paper towels from the dispenser and handed them to Theo. "Wrap it in this first so the cold doesn't damage your skin."

He said it in his usual calm tone, but Theo thought he could hear something in the voice. Disappointment? Not about the fight, but about Theo not knowing something as simple as needing to wrap something frozen before applying it his face. Scientifically, Theo knew that. Water freezes at thirty-two degrees Fahrenheit, but the bag of corn would probably be much colder. Applying it directly to his cheek could freeze the fluids and tissues in the skin and lead to frostbite. Severe frostbite could result in the loss of skin and muscle. Theo's School Brain knew all this, but his Everyday Brain hadn't been exposed to the usual sprained ankles and jammed fingers that most kids his age had suffered. He'd never used an ice pack before. He'd always considered himself lucky that he hadn't had those injuries. Now he wasn't so sure. Maybe the experiences would have been useful. Painful, but useful.

"Okay, nursing time is over," his dad said. "We've got us a dinner to cook."

"But I've got to ice my cheek." It was worth a try.

His dad opened a drawer and pulled out a roll of gray duct tape. "We could tape that bag to your face. That'll free up your hands." He pulled a couple of inches from the roll. "We just wrap this twice around your head, thing won't budge."

"Ha ha. Just tell me what you want me to do."

His dad grinned and put the tape away. He threw his arm around Theo's shoulder and gave him a squeeze. "There's my helpful son."

Theo didn't know if other fathers hugged their sons as much as his dad did. Or whether they leaned over and kissed the tops of their heads when they were sitting down doing homework. Or whether they randomly grabbed them by the necks and said, "My boy! My boy!" His dad did. And though sometimes Theo felt a little embarrassed by it, he didn't necessarily want it to stop.

"What are we making?" Theo asked, fetching the milk, butter, and eggs that his dad requested.

"I've got a better question," his dad said. "What was your fight about?"

Theo gulped. Yup, things just got worse.

"YOU didn't punch him back?" his dad asked while grating cheese.

"No."

"And the bloody nose was an accident? You're sure?"

"Yes."

"You apologized, right?"

"Yes."

His dad continued to grate cheddar cheese on top of the casserole. Theo continued to slice tomatoes, cucumbers, and mushrooms for the salad. Neither looked at the other, they just focused on their jobs like they were safecrackers trying to break into a particularly tough safe.

"And that's the whole story. That's everything?" his dad asked.

Theo hesitated. "Pretty much."

His dad nodded. Grated. Nodded.

"Pretty much" was the truth, but not the whole truth. Theo had left out the part about meeting Crazy Girl and Motorcycle Guy. The loud slap. The mysterious conversation

("This is your last chance!" he'd yelled. Last chance for what?). Theo wasn't sure why he didn't tell his dad. He'd always told his dad everything, especially after his mom died. When that happened, his dad suddenly needed to know every boring detail of Theo's daily life. Theo knew it wasn't because his dad was nosy, but because all the dull descriptions of Theo's routine in school made his dad feel like things were getting back to normal. A life-goes-on kind of thing. Every time Theo described a tricky problem from algebra class or a dreary discussion about the causes of the Civil War from social studies, he could see his dad relaxing, breathing easier—healing. Telling him made Theo feel better, too.

But for some unknown reason, today Theo didn't want to tell his dad everything. Any more than he'd wanted to tell Brian some of his recent thoughts. He was starting to see how his new height brought certain respect from some people. The problem was, that respect was unearned. All Theo had done was grow. Like a plant. No talent required. Yet people expected more of him. Theo was as big as an adult, so now suddenly he was supposed to act like one. So, he figured that along with those unwanted expectations should come a few cool privileges. Like keeping some stuff to himself. He didn't want to call them "secrets" exactly, because that seemed too much like lying. He preferred to think of it as a "secret identity." Growing was his super-power, so he needed a secret identity while he figured out where he fit in now that the world saw him differently.

His dad now sprinkled fried onion bits on top of the casserole. Brown flakes fell like snow.

The IKEA clock over the sink ticked loudly.

The silence was making Theo uncomfortable, like an itch. He was starting to feel guilty about not telling his dad everything that had happened. Maybe his whole "secret identity" thing was a load of crap. He was just about to confess when his dad spoke.

"Sorry, I missed your game, T-bird," his dad said. He looked over at Theo. "Won't happen again."

"Not a big deal. Like I said, I wasn't very good."

"It was only your first game. Give yourself some time. My first game on a team"—he stopped sprinkling and chuckled at the memory—"I got so excited when I intercepted a pass that I ran down the whole court and made a sweet reverse layup."

"Yeah, not really seeing how that helps."

"I made the layup in the *wrong* basket. I scored two points for the other team."

Theo nodded. His dad was always sharing these stories about how he made mistakes and screwed up and failed at things, but they never helped Theo feel better. His dad had been a star football player in high school and college. He didn't talk much about that. But there it was, the unspoken punch line to all his stories about messing up: he still ended up a hero.

"I would've played better if those kids in the bleachers

hadn't been hassling me," Theo said. "Talking about my skin and stuff."

Theo's dad put the can of onion bits down and frowned at Theo. "Feed the BIB," he said, pointing at an old mayonnaise jar half filled with dollar bills and change. A piece of masking tape was stuck to it with BIB written in black Magic Marker. His mother's handwriting.

"I wasn't saying *that*," Theo protested. "I was just—"

"Feed the BIB," his dad repeated, sliding the casserole into the oven.

Theo dug into his pocket and counted out a dollar in change. He dumped the coins into the jar.

His mother had started the BIB jar when Theo was ten and had come home with his sixth-grade report card. He had gotten a two (out of four) in physical education. Everything else was a four. Even though his parents had told him it was no big deal and they were very proud of him, Theo had stormed around the house complaining that the teacher gave him a bad grade because Theo was black and so everyone expected him to be a better athlete. Without a moment's hesitation, Theo's mom had pulled the jar out of the recycle bin, slapped on the label, and told him to go take a dollar out of his Batman bank. "Every time you make the excuse 'Because I'm Black,' you're putting a dollar in this jar."

"That's not fair!" Theo had hollered. "I'm not the one who's racist."

"Your teacher sent me an e-mail saying that you didn't

want to play soccer with the other kids. You kept walking off the field."

"I don't like soccer. It's stupid. Plus, the kids are always 'accidentally' kicking each other when they miss the ball."

"Not the point," his mom said. "You refused to play, so you got a two. Nothing to do with being black. More to do with being stubborn or lazy or scared. You pick."

Theo had placed his dollar in the jar.

"Sometimes," his mom said, "you will get the short end of the stick because you're black. People won't always say something to your face, but you'll know. You learn to see the signs. When that happens—"

"I get my money back?" Theo interrupted.

She laughed. "No. When that happens, I still don't want you to make excuses. Most people get discriminated against sometime in their lives. Because of their religion or gender, because they're too old or too young, too fat or too thin. Too pretty or too ugly. For some folks, other people are always going to be too something or other. You can't let that stop you from moving ahead. There's no shortage of excuses for not doing your best." She kissed his cheek. "Okay, lecture over."

"Finally," he teased. He looked at his lone dollar bill in the jar. Tried to figure how many dollar bills the jar would hold. A lot. "What are you going to do with the money? When it's full."

"I'm hoping it doesn't get full. Or it wouldn't be much of a lesson."

"Come on. Just in case. What if. What'll we spend it on?"

She smiled that big smile that showed off all her perfect teeth. "That's my secret."

Even his dad didn't know what she'd planned to use the money for, so they just left it in the jar. Neither of them wanted the jar to get full, because then they'd have to decide.

At least Theo wasn't the only one to put money in the jar. When his dad complained about being passed over for a promotion because he was "a little too tan" for some of the brass in the department, Theo's mom had made him put a dollar in the jar. Even his mom had put in a few dollars. Once, when a plumber charged her two hundred dollars for fixing a broken toilet, she'd claimed that he'd overcharged her because she was a woman. Theo's dad had held out the jar. "Feed the BIB," he'd insisted.

"But this was because I was a *woman*," she'd protested.

"Close enough," his dad had said with a grin.

She put a dollar in the jar. "Clearly you two are discriminating against me because I'm the mom."

"Feed the BIB!" Theo and his dad had chorused. His mom had laughed. And put another dollar in.

Theo looked at the jar, remembering her laugh. Not dainty, but a loud rising sound, like running your finger across all the keys of a piano, from low to high. Not like Crazy Girl's metallic laugh.

"Did you enjoy playing?" Theo's dad said.

"What?" Theo snapped back to the present. Casserole. Salad. Secret identity.

"Basketball. Did you at least enjoy playing with the rest of the guys? Being on a team and such?"

Theo shrugged. "Kinda."

"Forget the outcome, who won or lost. Forget your mistakes. When you were on the court, running back and forth, were you happy?"

"I don't know," he said instantly, but he did know. Despite the fear and embarrassment, he had liked being on the court. The excitement of not knowing what would happen next. People watching him. Running with the other boys on the team. He had been outside his thoughts and worries—about Mom, about Dad, about school. He'd been happy. "Yeah, I guess," Theo added. "It was all right."

But if he was being honest—really honest—it was probably the most exciting thing he'd ever done in his life. The fact that he sucked at it didn't change that fact at all.

And that scared him. To want to do something you weren't good at was begging to be let down. It was like telling a bully to please be careful with that squirt gun because you're wearing your favorite clothes.

"I forgot to tell you," his dad said too casually, in that way that said he hadn't forgotten but just didn't want to tell him. "We're driving up to Los Angeles to visit Grandma tomorrow."

Theo groaned. "Aw, why?"

His dad's voice got stern and lecture-y. "Because she's my mother and your grandmother. That's reason enough."

"I didn't mean it that way. I love Grandma. It's just that I'm so far behind on everything. And I was going to hang with Brian." Desperate, he pulled out the schoolwork card. "Plus, I've got to prepare for Aca-lympics." What parent can resist their child's plea to do *more* homework?

No sale. His dad gave him a withering look that announced End of Discussion.

Theo sighed. It wasn't visiting his grandma that annoyed him. He really did love her. She was funny and smart and let him eat whatever he wanted without a lecture about health. The annoying part was seeing his cousin Gavin.

Gavin.

Just thinking the name made Theo shudder. It was like sitting down to a dinner you knew was going to make you throw up. Theo hated Gavin. Not just hated—that was too mild. Gavin was to Theo what sunlight is to vampires. What soap was to Pigpen. What health food was to Homer Simpson.

At fifteen, Gavin was fourteen months older than Theo, and he thought he was the coolest guy who had ever lived. He was always bragging about his stylish clothes (which he claimed everyone always complimented), his awesome dancing (which he claimed everyone always wanted to learn), his music collection ("Twenty-five thousand songs and counting, son"), his hip-hop songs, which he wrote and never played for anyone but which would one day make him a multimillionaire hanging out with Kanye and Beyoncé.

Last time Theo had visited, Gavin had spent the whole time talking about what his stage name would be. "I need something kick-ass, something really *street*, ya know? Like 50 Cent or Big Rich or Bounty Killer. Those guys are tight. What do you think, Theo? You're supposed to be a big brain." Like that. For *two* days.

Gavin lived with Grandma Esther while his mom, Aunt Talia (Theo's dad's sister), was working in Africa for some nonprofit group. She had been there for two months. Theo and his dad had Skyped her last week and she'd walked her computer around to show them the African village where she was staying. She'd even introduced a couple of young village girls in brightly colored dresses who'd smiled and waved shyly. In the middle of their conversation, her Internet connection had gone dead, as it usually did where she was.

For the millionth time Theo wondered how such intelligent, selfless women like his aunt and grandmother could raise such a selfish poser as Gavin.

Theo shook his head and groaned. Worst Friday ever.

HIS dad set the timer for the casserole. Forty-five minutes. "Go ahead and stick the salad back in the fridge so it stays fresh."

Theo did. His dad helped him clean up the mess. Cucumber peels were stuffed into the garbage disposal. Mushy tomato guts were swept into the sink. When they were done, the kitchen was shining like new. His dad snapped on the oven light to check the casserole. He smiled like a fisherman who's just landed a record-breaking marlin.

Since Theo's mom's death, his dad had become a little obsessed with preparing Theo for the world. Cooking, cleaning, laundry—even ironing—their daily routine was like some sort of household boot camp. Whenever Theo complained, his dad gave the same speech: "You've got to be self-reliant, son. Be able to take care of yourself. What are you going to do when you're out living on your own?" He acted as if he were sending Theo off to war instead of the college he'd eventually be attending.

Here's why:

For almost six months after his mom's death, Theo and his dad had let everything in the house deteriorate. After they had eaten all the lasagna, sandwiches, and casseroles that friends and neighbors had provided following the funeral, they ate out. Fast food mostly. They would drive in, yell their order into a paint-chipped metal box, drive home in silence, and then eat in front of the TV in silence. Crumpled bags, cardboard french-fry trays, and ketchup-stained paper wrappers decorated the house like some new holiday dedicated to greasy food. Laundry was done only when they ran out of clothes and were hunting through the dirty piles for something that didn't smell too bad. The line for what smelled "too bad" kept getting moved.

It was great!

Then one day his dad came home with a couple of grocery bags of laundry detergent and household cleaners, sponges, and paper towels. Another couple of bags were filled with fresh fruit, vegetables, and steaks. His dad took out one of Mom's cookbooks, and together they learned how to prepare a meal. Later, they learned how to clean. And do laundry.

It sucked.

But after a couple months, Theo got used to it. He still grumbled about all the work, but there was something comforting about the routine. Sometimes he even laughed. Like when he watched his big muscular dad delicately pouring the inside of an egg back and forth between two halves of an eggshell so he could get just the egg white for a recipe. Mom had always done all that kind of stuff without Theo ever noticing. Now that he realized how hard she'd worked for them, he wished he could thank her. Instead, he helped his dad and hoped that counted for something.

His dad stirred the green beans in the frying pan, sprinkled some sliced almonds over them.

"More almonds," Theo said. The almonds made the green beans easier to eat. Theo was not a fan of vegetables unless they were combined with something sweet: marsh-mallows with yams, Craisins with spinach salad.

His dad grabbed more almonds and added them to the beans.

After dinner, Theo went to his room to finish his home-work. He'd done most of it at school, so it didn't take long. He thought about playing a quick game of Call of Duty, but it was late and he had to get up early for the drive to L.A. Plus, his body hurt from playing basketball twice in the same day. Not to mention getting punched in the face.

He went to the bathroom to brush his teeth and saw a small sunburst of red spotting his face. A gift from Jeremy's knuckles. The punch had only glanced off Theo's cheek. He tried to imagine the damage, and pain, if the fist had really connected. Mostly he hoped it would be gone by Monday so he wouldn't have to explain to his friends at school what had happened. Especially Brian, who would give him I-told-you-so looks for the rest of the week.

Theo's phone buzzed. He checked the screen. Brian. As if he'd known Theo was thinking deceptive thoughts about him.

"Hey," Theo said.

"What's the plan for tomorrow? Movie? Comic-book store? Zombie apocalypse?"

Theo explained about having to go to his grandmother's.

"Ugh. Gavin," Brian said. He'd met Gavin a couple years ago, at Thanksgiving. Gavin had called Brian "Butterball" the whole time, because "He's as plump as the turkey we're gonna eat." When Theo had defended his friend in front of the family, Gavin laughed it off as a joke. Later, after they'd all left, Theo had found one of his school notebooks torn to shreds and stuffed in the trash.

"How'd things go at Ground Zero?" Brian asked.

"What?" Theo asked.

"The basketball courts at Palisades."

"It was okay. No wedgies in sight."

"Make any new friends?" Brian asked, a hint of a smirk in his voice.

"Yeah. We're all going to the movies next week in matching Justin Bieber T-shirts."

They both laughed. But Theo felt guilty about not telling Brian the truth about the fight. Crazy Girl. Motorcycle Guy.

They talked awhile about a couple girls at school who seemed to be developing faster than the others. And about their favorite zombie television show, *The Walking Dead*, wondering which main character would be killed off next. Brian told Theo to call him when he got back from L.A., and Theo said he would.

Theo went to bed, but he couldn't fall asleep. Too much had happened, and images from the day just kept flying through his mind like a deck of cards tossed up in the air. He flipped on the light, wide-awake. He knew he should study science facts for the upcoming Aca-lympics competition. Since he'd started playing basketball, he'd fallen behind in his preparation. Instead, he propped open his laptop and started reading about basketball. Strategies, basic skills, plays. He watched game highlights on YouTube. Especially Dr. J (Crazy Girl was right about him, he was awesome). Maybe, if he studied basketball enough, he'd get better at it. Like math.

Suddenly Theo heard something strange. His dad was talking on the phone. He looked at the clock. Almost midnight. His dad was never on the phone this late. Theo's stomach clenched. Was there some sort of police emergency? Was his dad going to be called out to someplace dangerous?

Theo slid quietly out of bed, crept to the bedroom door, opened it a crack, and listened. His dad sounded frustrated and upset.

". . . I tried. It's just not working out. . . . No, I'm not going to say that. I don't care. . . . This is stupid, a bad idea. I'm sorry I let you talk me into it. . . ."

Then his voice got lower and Theo couldn't make out

what he was saying. But he could hear typing on a keyboard. His dad was talking on the phone while using a computer. Two things he hated to do separately, let alone at the same time.

Theo went back to bed, but he couldn't sleep. What was his dad so upset about?

A few minutes later, his dad shuffled down the hallway to his bedroom.

Theo waited half an hour. His dad usually fell asleep quickly. But he was a light sleeper, had been since Theo's mother died. It was as if he thought he had to be always ready to jump up in case of an emergency. Like he blamed himself for not protecting Mom, even though he hadn't been there when the car crash happened. Even if he had, how could he have stopped a drunk driver from running a red light?

Theo poked his head out into the hall. Listened. His dad snored.

He tiptoed past his father's door and down the stairs. He stepped over the two stairs that creaked and slipped into his dad's study. The computer was asleep, but not off, so it quickly popped open to the desktop photo of ten-year-old Theo running with his mother into the waves at Newport Beach. Theo lingered on the photo a moment before typing in his dad's password: Angelatheo3. Theo had figured that out a couple years ago after only ten minutes. His mom's name, Theo's name, and the three of them as a family.

Theo hesitated. Who was this kid suddenly breaking into his father's computer? What was happening to him? Growing a few inches couldn't explain all this. What kind of crazy thing might he do next? He was actually kind of scared to find out.

But that didn't stop him.

Theo checked his dad's history. He clicked on the most recent site: Why Wait Mate.

A dating site!

The screen filled with a profile page of his dad: Marcus Rollins. There was a photo of him, taken with the computer camera, looking stiff and nervous. Like a wanted poster. He was looking for a woman who liked to stay active, loved children, and appreciated conversation. Favorite music: *Anything Motown, especially Stevie Wonder and Marvin Gaye. Also, songs by Joni Mitchell.*

Joni Mitchell? Who was that? How could it be that Theo didn't know that about his dad but strangers would?

About Family: *Just me and my son, Theo, 13 going on 25. He's smart, funny, loving. I couldn't have wished for a more perfect son.*

Theo's face burned with shame. A perfect criminal.

"Theo?" His dad's sleepy voice echoed from upstairs. "You up?"

"Yes, Dad. Just getting some water."

"Okay." Pause. "You all right?"

"Fine, Dad. Just thirsty."

His dad's concern, even when only half awake, made

Theo feel even guiltier. Not to mention he was adding lying to spying. Some "perfect son" he'd turned out to be.

On the other hand, his dad should have told him about this whole online dating thing. Was he shopping for a new wife? A mother for Theo? Theo had a right to know.

It looked like Theo wasn't the only one with a secret identity. Theo would have to keep an eye on him.

"CIGARETTE?" Gavin asked, expertly shaking his pack so a single cigarette poked out about an inch. He offered it to Theo.

They were walking to the park to shoot baskets while Theo's dad and Grandma Esther made lunch and argued about politics.

"Pass," Theo said, waving the pack away.

"Still playing the role of Good Negro." Gavin said "Negro" sarcastically, which Theo guessed was the only way anyone said that word these days.

"I'm not playing any role, Gavin. I just don't want to suck on a burning stick stuffed with poison. Especially just because a bunch of wrinkly old white dudes in shiny suits who never were cool a single day in their lives tell me that it's the cool thing to do. Feel me?"

Gavin laughed. "Yeah, I feel you, little cousin."

Gavin had been calling Theo "little cousin" since they were little kids, even though Theo was now half a foot taller. However, Gavin was about forty pounds heavier than Theo, and every single one of those pounds was chiseled muscle. The muscles were even bigger than the last time Theo had seen him. His biceps strained against the sleeves of his too-tight black T-shirt. When he walked, his pecs shifted around as if he had ferrets under his skin fighting to break out.

"What's with the muscle-head thing?" Theo asked. "You on steroids?"

"I don't need steroids, just hard work. Grandma bought me a set of used weights at a yard sale. Plus I do sit-ups and push-ups three times day." He dropped to the ground and did ten perfect push-ups. He jumped up and grinned. "Your turn."

"What's the point?" Theo said dismissively, though he was a little jealous.

"Showbiz, cuz, and simple mathematics. LL Cool, Kanye. All those guys perform with their shirts off. Girls go thermal. Sells downloads. I'm getting ready for my career as a world-famous recording artist. Kinda like you studying for your SATs." He looked over Theo's skinny body and laughed. "I can show you how to bulk up some. Right now you look like a strong fart will send you into orbit." He stuck a cigarette between his lips and lit it.

Theo didn't like the way Gavin had made him feel like a little kid so easily, so he started in again with what he knew best: facts. He pointed at Gavin's cigarette. "Did you know that there are over four thousand chemicals in tobacco smoke, sixty-nine of which cause cancer? Each cigarette contains chemicals found in batteries, industrial solvents, insecticide, toilet cleaner, sewer gas, and rocket fuel."

"Rocket fuel?" Gavin nodded, pleased. "Guess that's why I like it so much. Gives me energy. Better than Red Bull." He took a deep drag on his cigarette and blew the smoke out. "Or it could be the sewer gas. I'll get back to you on that."

That was Gavin. Never took anything seriously.

Theo ignored him, bouncing the basketball as they walked. On every previous visit, Gavin had tried to get Theo to go to the neighborhood park to play basketball. Theo usually refused. For one thing, Gavin's friends thought it was great fun to pick on Theo. For another, Gavin was always suggesting things that could get them in trouble. The last time he'd tried to talk Theo into getting a tattoo with him. "Or better yet," he'd said, "we should get branded. That's really badass."

"Branded? As in shoving hot metal against your skin until it fries?"

Gavin had nodded enthusiastically. "I hear your skin smells like bacon."

"Isn't that what they used to do to slaves?"

Gavin had retorted, "It's what slaves had done *to* them. This is a choice."

"Yeah," Theo had scoffed, "a really dumb choice. Plus, your mom and Grandma would kill you."

"Once it's done, nothing they can do about it."

That was Gavin, too. Acted like he didn't care what

anyone thought. Yet Theo noticed he had no brand or tattoo, nor had he had his name shaved into his hair or lines shaved into his eyebrows like he'd also talked about doing. He was mostly bluster.

Theo dribbled the ball harder, faster. This time he felt ready to face Gavin's friends: he was taller and knew a few more moves. And he needed the practice. Since Coach Mandrake announced that Theo was going to be the core of the team's offense, Theo felt like he should be practicing every moment.

"So you're on the basketball team now, huh?" Gavin said.

"Yeah."

"They teach you anything useful?"

"Guess we'll find out," Theo said, hoping he sounded cool and confident.

Suddenly Gavin snatched the ball from Theo's hands and ran ten feet in front of him. His cigarette dangled from his lips while he dribbled. "Guess they didn't teach you how to hold on to the ball at your white school."

"It's not a white school. In fact, whites are the minority. The principal is Asian."

"Always with the facts and stats. It's not about the number of whites, it's about the attitude, son. Don't you get that? Even if it isn't mostly white, they're still teaching you to be white."

"What does that even mean?"

"Fancy computers and SMART Boards and all that junk is just meant to make you a mindless consumer. Ya gotta stay true to who you are, son."

"Like you? A gangsta wannabe who's failing at school and who's probably going to be stacking boxes at Costco the rest of his life?"

"See, that right there is white attitude. Nothing wrong with honest hard work."

"I didn't say there was. I just said that you don't have to limit your opportunities just because you're lazy. All your race crap is an excuse for you to do nothing but lift weights. Try lifting a book once in a while."

Gavin frowned and flicked his cigarette in Theo's direction but not really at him. "You could always talk, little cousin. I'll give you that." He started dribbling the ball across the street to the park. "Let's see how much good talk does you here."

Theo followed him across the street, through the park, and to the basketball courts. The park wasn't as nice as Palisades Park. There were a few brown patches of dirt where there used to be grass; some of the trees looked worn down, like they'd been climbed often and roughly. The basketball courts were also more worn: the pavement had long, jagged cracks, making the surface look like it was divided into continents. The line paint was faded and chipped. The nets sagging from the rims were torn, and one rim had no net.

A group of four guys, all black, waved at Gavin and called his name. That was another thing that was different: most of the people in the park were black, like the neighborhood. Theo's park and neighborhood were models of ethnic diversity, with whites, Hispanics, Asians, Indians, Muslims, and even a few Sikh guys in turbans. Sometimes Theo thought the place was like a movie set for some futuristic America where everyone got along. But here, nearly every face was some shade of black. Gavin had once asked Theo if being here "among his own" made him feel more at home. It didn't. He didn't feel intimidated either.

Gavin introduced Theo to the other players. Then, without any small talk, they jumped right into playing. The play was different than at Palisades Park. More fancy dribbling. More fouling. More shoving.

More trash talk:

"Take off your skirt and play like a man."

"You call that guarding? I wouldn't let you guard my fries at lunch."

"You need GPS to find the basket, son."

A couple of others that were way more colorful.

And several that involved body parts in unusual situations.

More than a few of these comments were directed at Theo.

Gavin was on the other team, of course, and volunteered to guard Theo. He played rough, but no rougher than the other kids. A teammate would lob the ball to Theo for an inside layup and someone would jump up to block, slamming Theo just enough so he'd miss the shot. The first time, Theo let it go. The second time, he called a foul, but everyone just laughed, even his own teammates. "No blood, no foul," they said.

They didn't really mean that, because a few plays later Theo got knocked down by one of the players and skinned his elbow. Blood seeped through the shredded skin. But still, no foul.

"You need an ambulance, little cousin?" Gavin smirked, helping him to his feet.

"I'm fine, dude."

"In case you haven't noticed, no one around here says 'dude.' That's surfer talk, *dude*."

Theo continued to play, getting elbowed in the ribs, stomped on both feet, hip-checked in the crotch (*that* felt like he might need an ambulance). After about an hour, Gavin told them he had to leave. Theo said nothing, but he was relieved. He felt as battered as if he'd been whirled in a blender. The rest of the guys complained and tried to talk Gavin into staying, but he pointed at Theo and shrugged, as if to say, "I'm babysitting, nothing I can do."

On the walk home, Theo said, "You didn't have to quit on my account. I was doing fine."

Gavin snorted. "I don't want Uncle Marcus giving me a hard time about his baby boy getting hurt."

"Did you hear me complain?"

"Nope. And you surprised me with some skills. Still, you're like a toddler wandering into traffic. Not one of the real players."

"Real players? All they did was shove and foul. In a real game they'd all have fouled out."

"That was a real game. What real game are you talking about?"

"In a gym, with referees."

"That's just one kind of 'real' game. Not the only kind."

"Oh, I see. It's not a real game when you have to play by the rules. Right, gangsta?" Theo said "gangsta" as sarcastically as Gavin had said "dude."

Theo expected Gavin to get angry. But he didn't. That was new.

Gavin laughed. "Look, I'm just saying, your problem is you don't play basketball to win. You play to not look stupid."

Theo stopped walking. He could feel his skin heating up with anger. His cheeks actually burned. "What are you talking about?"

"The way I see it, little cousin, there are three types of jammers. First, you got your average player with no particular talent who enjoys hanging with his boys. That's me. I can play okay, but the game don't mean nothing to me. Win or lose, same deal to me. Next, you got your guys who are always watching the clock or the score or whatever, just praying for the game to be finished because they think everyone's judging them every second. They're panicking the whole time they're on the court, thinking they don't have what it takes. That's you, man. Finally, you got those who never want the game to be over, because each minute is like living on some planet where you got no problems. They feel like they're flying, or driving a hundred miles an hour with no chance of crashing. Winning for them isn't even a question. They know every time they grab a ball that they're going to win. Even when they don't win, they still feel like they did, because they were, for that brief time, in a place where everything they thought or did mattered. That's who you *wish* you were."

Theo grabbed the ball out of Gavin's hands and started home alone. "You see me maybe once every six months and you think you know all about me. You don't know anything."

Gavin didn't say anything. No dig, no joke, no insult. That, too, was new.

"ISN'T this game too white for you?" Theo asked sarcastically. Since they'd arrived back at Grandma Esther's house, everything Theo had said to Gavin was snide. He knew he was acting childishly, but he couldn't seem to stop himself. There was a gnawing in his stomach that only sarcasm seemed to soothe.

Gavin laughed. "Only color I'm interested in right now is red. As in blood." They were playing Call of Duty in Gavin's room. The room was a mess, with dumbbells scattered in one corner, a desk buried under comic books and dirty clothes in another, the TV and video games in a third, and his piano keyboard and computer in the fourth. The keyboard and computer were where Gavin supposedly wrote his music. For years he had been telling everyone what a major hip-hop star he was going to be one day, only he never let anyone hear any of his songs.

Theo had considered sulking by himself, but his dad would soon have pulled him into the kitchen to look at photo albums, mostly filled with faded Polaroids of his grandmother in low-cut, slinky outfits from back when she was a popular blues and jazz singer (she'd actually made a few albums). People always expected his grandma to look like some short, chubby version of Madea, in a flowery housedress and apron, always laughing and calling people "folks" or "child" ("You folks jes set yoselves down. Ain't that right, child?").

But Grandma was slim, dressed in jeans and flannel shirts, and had thick black-and-gray dreadlocks that hung to her butt. She divided her days between visiting her old musician friends and participating in her various political activities. Back in the sixties, she'd been involved in some radical protests. Now she just wanted to make sure everybody got a chance to vote. Theo had heard all the stories, seen all the yellowish photos, heard Grandma's political speeches. He'd rather shoot zombie Nazis, even if it was with Gavin.

He looked at the clock. He just had to endure Gavin for another hour and then they'd be heading back to Orange County.

"You suck at this," Gavin said as he mowed down half a dozen soldiers. His score was twice Theo's.

"When's your mom coming back?" Theo asked. He was sorry the moment he heard his own words. He already knew the answer, but he just wanted to rub it in, hurt Gavin a little.

"Six weeks," Gavin said without any emotion.

Gavin's mom had caught the whole political activist bug from Grandma. She married some guy who was a big shot in the Peace Corps. But a year after Gavin was born, her husband took off to do some rescue work in Thailand after a hurricane. He never came back. He didn't die, he just preferred going from disaster area to disaster area rather than raising his son. He still sent e-mails from all over the world. Theo didn't know whether Gavin ever responded. They never talked about him.

His mom was in Kenya, installing "smart" hand pumps in villages. She'd explained the project to Theo once. "Millions of people in Africa get all their water from hand pumps—you know, the kind you see in westerns when the cowboy rides up to the farm and asks if he can have some water, then sticks his head under the faucet and starts pumping. The problem is that they break down a lot. About a third of the pumps are broken at any given time," she'd said. "My company invented a mobile data transmitter that gets implanted into the pump handle. When the pump doesn't work, it sends a text message, and we go and fix the pump."

Theo admired Aunt Talia. She was actually doing something to make the world better. Not just talking about fame and fortune, like her son, Gavin.

Gavin suddenly broke the silence. "This is her last trip. She said she misses me too much and she doesn't want to turn into my dad. We Skype a lot."

"That's good," Theo said, suddenly feeling bad for Gavin. Not to mention himself. At least Gavin's mom would be coming home eventually. Theo wouldn't be so lucky.

As if sensing Theo's change of mood, Gavin spun and glared at him. "None of this matters anyway. When my songs catch on, I'm going to be outta here, living in some big white mansion in Beverly Hills. Maybe I'll let you come visit, take a dip in my pool with all the hot chicks. Swimming suit optional." He laughed as nastily as he could.

"Yeah, right," Theo said. "Your 'music.'" He said "music" like he was saying "unicorn."

"Got some tight tunes, son. You'll see."

"If your songs are so tight, why not play some for me right now? Go ahead. Right now."

Gavin's chest swelled with anger, and Theo wondered if he was going to punch him. Theo hoped not, because those arms were massive. And he was already sore from the beating he had taken playing basketball with Gavin's friends.

Gavin turned back to the game and rebooted it. He played silently by himself while Theo watched the clock for his dad to come take him away.

"THAT wasn't so bad, right?" his dad said on the drive home. "A little face time with family didn't kill you."

"It was okay," Theo said. He hoped that would be enough for his dad. He really didn't feel like talking about Gavin.

"So, T-bone," his dad said, "what's the best thing that happened yesterday? I forgot to ask last night."

During the school week, Marcus always asked at dinner, "What's the best thing that happened to you today?" That way he kept up on Theo's life in school.

The question wasn't a surprise to Theo. What was a surprise was what popped into his head.

Crazy Girl.

He thought of her walking next to him at the court, spinning the ball on her finger. Calling him Sasquatch (which actually was kinda funny, though he'd never admit that to her). The way she took that slap from Motorcycle Guy without crying, then stood up and fearlessly kicked him right in the shin.

"Son?" his dad prompted. "Too many choices?"

"Huh?"

"About the best thing that happened." He shook his head the way adults do whenever they want to say, "Teenagers. What airheads."

Theo was about to give his dad an answer he would find acceptable, like playing basketball, or getting an A on an algebra quiz. Girls weren't something he talked about with his dad. Too embarrassing. Sometimes Marcus would ask, "Any girls you think are cute at school?" Theo always shrugged. "Really?" his dad would persist. "No one? Not one girl in the entire school is attractive to you?" Theo would shrug again.

He'd perfected a variety of elaborate shrugs so expressive they could be a language all their own. "Are you just scared of talking to them?" his dad would ask. Shrug Number 8 (translation: Maybe a little). "You just have to ask them about themselves. What are their hobbies? What bands do they listen to? You play the guitar, so ask them if they play an instrument." Sigh and shrug Number 14 (translation: If you keep talking about this, I'll leave the room).

"What was the best thing that happened to *you* yesterday?" Theo asked his dad, hoping to dodge his own answer.

"Easy," Marcus said. "Same as every day. This. Hanging out with you."

Theo groaned. "We need to start another jar," he said. "The TC jar. Too Corny. Every time you say something too corny or too emo, you pop a dollar in the jar."

His dad laughed. "Too emo. Gotcha."

Marcus turned on the radio to an oldies station and sang along with the Eagles' "Hotel California."

Relieved that his dad had stopped prying, Theo stuck his hand into his backpack for his Aca-lympics study notes. He'd have to study every spare moment if he was going to have time for Coach Mandrake's master plan. As his fingers dug into the backpack, he found a CD wrapped in notebook paper. Handwritten on the disk was *Songs, Vol. 1.*

"What's that?" Marcus asked.

"I think it's Gavin's songs."

His dad laughed. "Really? I thought that was an urban myth, like albino alligators and healthy doughnuts."

"Me, too." Theo studied the disk. "And so low-tech. He could have just e-mailed me the song file."

"I guess he wanted it to be more private. Not something on a computer that anyone could access."

Theo felt his scalp tingle. Was his dad talking about Theo looking at the dating profile? Did he know? Theo looked at his dad's face for some sign but saw nothing.

"Let's play it," Marcus suggested.

"I've got to study, Dad." Theo wasn't in the mood for even one more second of Gavin, especially after feeling like he'd finally escaped.

"I'm curious. Aren't you?"

"Not really."

"He put it in your backpack for a reason, son."

"Fine." Theo sighed and stuck the CD in the player. Gavin started singing.

> *This is not the same old song*
> *Kids in the backseat while the parents*
> *get along*

"Huh," his dad said, sounding surprised. "Not a bad voice."

> *This is about how to stay alive when*
> *The kids are in the backseat and there's*
> *no one drivin'.*

Marcus nodded appreciatively. "I like the way he rhymes 'alive when' with 'drivin'.' Unexpected."

Theo made a grumbling sound.

When the first song was over, they listened to the other three.

Theo hated to admit it, but Gavin's voice *was* pretty good. Worse, his songs were also pretty good. If he was honest, Theo thought the songs were *really* good. One song was about missing his mom. Another was about the plight of the poor in Africa. Another was about neighborhood life in L.A. They all had catchy tunes, but they were also touching. Theo had expected harsh hip-hop about chicks, guns, and violence. He hadn't realized Gavin had this side to him.

"Sorry, T-Rex," his dad said sympathetically.

"What for?"

"I know you and Gavin have always butted heads. Now the little punk goes and writes these terrific songs. That's got to burn you up."

"Do I seem that shallow?" Theo asked.

"We're all that shallow sometimes. Part of human frailty."

"I'm glad they're good," Theo said. He'd said that just for his dad's sake. He knew that's how he should feel. What he actually felt was anger and jealousy.

He ejected the CD, stuck it in his backpack, and started studying for the Aca-lympics.

But his mind kept wandering back to Gavin's music. Apparently there was more to his cousin than bragging and showing off.

Then Theo thought about what Gavin had said to him when they were leaving the basketball court. Was he right about Theo playing just hard enough not to look foolish? Why *was* he playing basketball? For his dad? Did he think it would help his dad get over his mom faster? And why did he start the Aca-lympics? Was it because it made his mom proud? Or was it because Brian had talked him into it? Theo couldn't even remember.

This, more than Gavin's talent, was what was making him feel jealous: Gavin had found something he loved, and he was doing it for no one but himself. Did Theo do *anything* he cared enough about to fight for a win?

"HE'S lying," Tunes said, pointing at Theo. "Do you concur, Doctor?"

"I concur, Doctor." Daryl nodded. "The boy has a serious case of Big Fat Liar-itis. And I'm afraid it's spreading. Like peanut butter on a cracker."

"Like tomato sauce on a pizza."

"Like dog poop on a shoe."

"Is there a cure, Doctor?"

Daryl shook his head sadly. "I'm afraid not. It's terminal. Unless, of course, he decides to tell us the truth. That's his only chance to live. Do you concur, Doctor?"

"I concur," Tunes said.

Tunes and Daryl stared at Theo as if waiting for him to confess to selling nuclear secrets to China. Tunes and Daryl were big fans of the actor Leonardo DiCaprio, so they were constantly, and annoyingly, quoting his movies. ("I concur" came from *Catch Me If You Can*, in which Leo played a teenager pretending to be a real doctor and kept repeating "I concur" to other real doctors because he saw a doctor on a soap opera say it. Unbelievably, it worked.)

"You guys are idiots," Theo said.

"I do not concur," Daryl said.

"Nor I," Tunes said.

Daryl and Tunes high-fived each other and laughed.

"What do you think, Brookenstein?" Tunes asked. "Is our boy Theo a terminal liar?"

Brooke Hill was slouching at a desk on the other side of the classroom. She was studying a fat book on colonial American history. She wore a fuzzy black sweater with multicolored sequins that formed a large, elaborate *B* on her chest, a little like Superman's uniform. Everything she wore was fancy and glittery and expensive. She was the richest person in the school, the prettiest person in the school, and also the smartest person in the school. She looked up at Tunes's question, scanned all three boys as if looking at a display of repulsive insects, and returned to her reading.

These were the members of Brain Train, Orangetree Middle School's Aca-lympics team. The elite squad of straight-A eggheads and social shadow dwellers.

Gary Sanchez was called Tunes because he could identify almost any song ever written within the first few notes and quote all the lyrics. Didn't matter what kind of song—pop, classical, musical, opera, rap (even novelty songs like "Purple People Eater")—he knew them all. He was also an accomplished pianist who had already given a concert of classical music on a real stage for a paying audience. But he wasn't all I'm-into-Beethoven-so-I'm-cool. He and Theo had jammed a few times in Gary's garage, with Theo on guitar and Gary on keyboard (and Brian on the sofa), playing some down-and-dirty rock and roll, like Bruce Springsteen and Van Halen. After graduating from Orangetree, Gary was going to attend the local high school for performing arts. Naturally, his specialty on the Brain Train was the performing arts, including everything from music to stage to ballet. (Yes, even ballet, though Theo and the guys promised not to tease him about that. Too much.)

Daryl Tran was the team's math genius. He sometimes caught mistakes that Mr. Fielding, the algebra teacher, made in solving equations. In fact, he was so brilliant that Mr. Fielding didn't even mind when Daryl corrected him in front of the class, as if it was an honor, like Mr. Fielding was a weekend golfer getting a tip from Tiger Woods. Daryl was also taking an advanced calculus course at the local community college. He told the guys that the college girls in his class sometimes hit on him, but no one believed him, because whenever a girl came within five feet of him his face broke out into a rain-forest-level sweat. His parents owned a small Vietnamese restaurant that Daryl worked at every day after school. Sometimes the guys would visit him there and his parents would give them all free food. They seemed happy (and surprised) that Daryl had any friends at all.

Brooke specialized in American history, geography, and current events. She was the only member of the team who covered more than one subject. She didn't socialize with the rest of them. Once they'd invited her along to Daryl's restaurant. She'd snorted and walked out of the room as if they'd asked her to take off her clothes and run down the hall singing the national anthem. The weird thing about Brooke was that, although she was smart and rich and attractive, she didn't seem to have any friends. Not one. Not that people didn't try. Especially all the popular Bees (short for wannabes) that buzzed around her looking for an invitation to her mansion, where, it was rumored, she had an enormous swimming pool with a waterfall and slide, and a Jacuzzi as big as the pool. For some reason no one could figure out, Brooke ignored everyone.

"Sorrysorrysorry. Sorry I'm late!" Brian burst into the room, panting and sweating. "What'd I miss? What'd I miss?" He clumsily ran into a desk, knocking it into a couple other desks. "Owww!"

The final member of Brain Train. Specialty: literature and art.

"You didn't miss anything," Theo said. "Mr. J isn't here yet."

Brian collapsed into a seat. "Excellent."

"Wait a minute," Tunes said with a grin. "You did in fact miss something. Something very important. You missed Theo here telling us all about the brutal fistfight he got into at the park. Broken teeth were flying everywhere."

Daryl laughed. "Yeah. He Chuck Norris'd some poor Asian kid. Sounds like a hate crime to me. Do you concur?"

Tunes nodded. "I concur."

"He's even got a bruise on his cheek to prove it. Show him your war wound, Theo."

Theo sighed and turned his cheek toward Brian. The red splotch wasn't as bright as it had been two days ago, but it was still visible. Like a bug bite. From a tiny, tiny bug.

"The guy must have had marshmallows for fists," Daryl said.

"You sure that isn't rouge?" Tunes said. "My sister puts that on to make her cheeks red."

"Your sister looks like a clown," Daryl said.

"I concur," Tunes said.

"Wait a minute! Wait. A. Minute," Brian hollered. "You were in a *fight*?"

"Not just a fight," Tunes said. "He also came to the rescue of a hot girl—"

"I didn't say she was hot," Theo interrupted.

"It's implied," Daryl said.

"And," Tunes continued, "he confronted some sinister goon on a motorcycle."

"I think I read that story in *Artemis Fowl*," Daryl said. "Only this guy had magical powers. Did your guy have magical powers, Theo? Did he levitate the motorcycle or make cheese appear out of thin air?"

"What kind of cheese?" Tunes asked.

"Muenster is the traditional favorite of wizards and warlocks. Witches, on the other hand, prefer Tyrolean gray. From Austria."

"Fascinating," Tunes said.

They high-fived again and snickered.

"Pay no attention to these morons," Brian said. "The only adventure they have is putting rubber bands on their braces. What really happened?"

Theo told him. When he got to the part about Motorcycle Guy hitting Crazy Girl and Crazy Girl kicking him back, Brooke looked up for a moment. Without any change in expression, she returned to her reading.

"I told you that park was dangerous," Brian said. He looked at the others. "I told him. You never hang out where guys play sports. Their testosterone is already at dangerous levels. Add competitive sports into the mix? Recipe for violence."

"We should Yelp the park," Tunes said. "Warn people to stay away."

Theo wondered why he had bothered to tell them. At first, he'd been prepared to explain how he got his bruise, figuring they would ask him about it. But the bruise was hardly visible, so no one had. He went ahead and volunteered the story anyway while they waited for Mr. J. Which meant he was kind of proud of what had happened. He wanted them to know. Why? It's not like he actually did anything. He didn't confront Motorcycle Guy. He didn't save Crazy Girl. He didn't punch Asian Kid. But *something* had happened.

Something unpredictable and scary.

And he'd been there. In the middle of it.

"I can't believe you didn't call or text me about it," Brian said.

Theo was surprised to see that Brian was hurt. Probably because they usually told each other everything as soon as it happened. They'd been doing that since they were old enough to speak (and exaggerate). But, for some reason, Theo had wanted this to be just his story for a while. He'd wanted to savor it, examine it, try it on and see how this new Theo—the one in the middle of danger and drama—suited him. The only other drama in his life had been his mom's death, and after that everyone saw him as Poor Theo. He'd hated that. Bright eyes turning sad the moment he entered a room. This new Theo, taller and more daring, fit him better. Or at least he wanted it to.

"Is that why you didn't want to get together Sunday?" Brian asked.

Partially. Plus, he'd spent several hours shooting baskets at the park. He'd gone there early, before anyone else showed up. As soon as he saw kids approaching on their bikes with basketballs under their arms, he'd taken off. But he couldn't tell Brian that. "No, dude. I had homework to catch up on. The basketball team is taking up a lot of my time."

"We have a basketball team?" Daryl asked.

"That's debatable," Brian said, turning away from Theo.

Theo felt bad, but he promised himself he'd make it up to Brian later by telling him about his dad's computer dating secret. Brian would have a lot to say about that.

"Hey, what's this?" Tunes said. He'd picked up Gavin's CD from the floor next to Theo's open backpack.

"Nothing," Theo said, grabbing for it. He'd forgotten it was in there.

"Not so fast, Young Skywalker." Tunes ran over to the computer on Mr. J's desk. He slid the CD into the slot and tapped some keys.

Theo stood up and walked to the desk. "Come on, Tunes. Give it back."

"I want to hear what kind of music is so important to you that you carry it around on this ancient disc."

Daryl said, "Maybe it's a mix-tape for some girl." He said "girl" like it was a foreign word he'd just learned. "Probably all songs by Disney chicks like Selena Gomez and Demi Lovato."

Theo looked to Brian for help, but Brian pretended not to notice. Punishment for not confiding in him about what had happened at the park.

Suddenly Gavin's voice blew through the tinny computer speakers. After the first verse, Tunes grabbed his phone and started recording the song. The only musical accompaniment was a few keyboard chords here and there. During the song, no one spoke. Even Brooke looked up for a few seconds before returning to her studies.

When the first song was over, Theo ejected the CD and slid it back into the folded notebook paper.

"Hey, man," a voice called from the doorway. Three students were crowded around. "Who was that? It was awesome. Is it on iTunes?"

Theo shook his head. "No. Just a home recording by my cousin."

They shrugged and left.

"That was Gavin?" Brian asked in shock.

"Yeah," Theo admitted. He didn't want to discuss it anymore. He hated that everyone liked it so much. It was bad enough he had to see Gavin in L.A. He didn't want Gavin's presence spilling into his life here.

"The dude has talent," Tunes said. He held up his phone and started replaying the song. "I should post this on Facebook, see how many Likes he gets."

"No!" Theo said, trying to snatch the phone. "Come on, man. Don't. He'd kill me."

Daryl laughed. "Relax, dude. I'm just kidding. I wouldn't do that to you. We're a team, right? The Unstoppable Brain Train." He deleted the song. "See?"

"Right," Theo said. "Thanks."

But he was thinking that they didn't feel like a team. Not like when he was playing basketball. In basketball, there was all this silent movement, relying on the others to go where they were supposed to, to run out and help you when you were trapped. To feed you the ball when you were open. The Brain Train was five overachievers who didn't play well with others, answering questions as if they were by themselves at home in their rooms. How was that a team?

Just then, Mr. J appeared in the doorway holding a grocery bag. He grinned. "Now that music appreciation is over, who's ready for sudden death?"

EVERYONE scrambled to set up their chessboards, arranging the pieces as they had been left the last time they'd all played "sudden death." As Theo carefully placed the queen and rooks, he felt especially confident about his chances of finally beating Mr. J.

No one ever had. Yet.

"Tunes!" Mr. J suddenly barked, pointing at him. He then sang, "'I went to Kansas City on a Friday.' What's the next lyric? Go!"

"'By Saturday I learned a thang or two.' Title: 'Everything's Up to Date in Kansas City.' From the Rodgers and Hammerstein musical *Oklahoma!*"

"Very good. Now move."

Sudden death involved playing Mr. J in a game of chess while he shouted out questions from each kid's special area of knowledge. His theory was that if they could answer questions while concentrating on chess, they wouldn't feel as pressured in the real competition. It seemed to work. In their first Aca-lympic match of the season, two weeks ago against Fullerton, they'd won. Not just won, but crushed them into oblivion, 145–23. However, Fullerton was always a bottom-feeder team that rarely made the regional tournament, so he'd warned them not to get cocky.

Mr. J stood in front of Daryl's chessboard. Daryl finally moved his queen. Mr. J studied the pieces for three seconds, and then moved his knight. "Checkmate in six moves," he said, slapping the clock. Daryl frowned in disbelief as if he'd just been told he had an extra ear growing out of his neck.

"How? I've got your rook and both bishops and I'm closing in on your other rook."

Mr. J said, "Where does the word 'algebra' come from?"

Daryl looked up, confused.

Mr. J snapped his fingers. "Come on, come on, Daryl. This game is lost anyway. Focus on what you still can win."

"You're bluffing. Trying to rattle me because I'm about to beat you." He slid his queen across the board and knocked over Mr. J's rook. He looked up at Mr. J with a delighted grin. "Warned ya." He slapped the clock.

Mr. J instantly hopped his knight over Daryl's pawn. "Check. Next you're going to go here, since it's your only move." He tapped the square with his finger. "Then I go here, check again. You bring the rook in to threaten my knight, but I go here and . . . checkmate. In six." He knocked over Daryl's king. "Warned ya. Now, answer my question."

Daryl sighed in defeat. "'Algebra' comes from the Arabic *al-jebr*, meaning 'reunion of broken parts.'"

Mr. J shrugged. "Correct, but too late. You let yourself get distracted by personal thoughts of glory and forgot about the goal: answering the question."

"Yo, Mr. J," Brian said. "I think I've got you this time."

"Yo, Brian," Mr. J said, walking to his chessboard. "'No man is an island, entire of itself; every man is a piece of the continent.' Author and work?"

Brian absently chewed on a captured pawn. "Uh, John Donne. 'Meditation,' uh . . . 'Ten'?"

"Seventeen," Mr. J corrected. "And what famous novel takes its title from this poem?"

"Ernest Hemingway's *For Whom the Bell Tolls.*"

"'And therefore never send to know for whom the bell tolls; it tolls for thee.'" Mr. J slid a pawn forward one space and said, "Checkmate in eight moves."

"Crap!" Brian said, and started gnawing on the pawn again.

Mr. J clapped his hands loudly. "Anyone here order an extra-large can of whup-ass? 'Cuz that's exactly what Lansing Middle School is going to deliver to you five sitting in front of me. Any of you pretenders to the throne going to prove them wrong?"

No one said anything. Lansing had beaten Orangetree every year for the past eight years. They'd won the gold medal in the state Aca-lympics for the past three years. Theo had heard all kinds of stories about the effects Lansing had on their competitors. Opposing teams would get so intimidated that they'd forget even basic information.

Some kids burst into tears during matches. One guy peed himself when he forgot who'd assassinated Lincoln. All the members of the Turtle Rock Middle School team quit after getting stomped by Lansing, and one of them had started seeing a therapist. Another kid had stopped speaking altogether and only communicated through writing with purple crayons on yellow sticky notes. Theo didn't believe that one.

Mr. J shook his head at their silence. "Not exactly the rousing cheer of enthusiasm I had hoped for. Or is this a case of 'Men of few words are the best men'? What's that from, Brian?"

"Shakespeare's *Henry V*," Brian announced proudly, happy to redeem himself.

Mr. J opened the grocery bag on his desk and removed the contents: a six-pack of Coke and a bag of Snickers bars. "I smuggled in this contraband against state nutritional guidelines, common sense, and every rule of dental hygiene, because you guys are going to need a morning caffeine-and-sugar jolt to get through the next hour of practice." He handed out the Cokes and Snickers bars. "Let me assure you, lady and gentlemen, there will be blood!"

Everyone ripped into their snack. Even Brooke.

Clinton Jacobson was Orangetree's STEM teacher (Science, Technology, Engineering, and Mathematics) as well as the Brain Train's faculty adviser. On the wall behind his desk was a poster of Albert Einstein sticking out his tongue. That kind of summed up Mr. J: he didn't seem to take much seriously, and he was the smartest person any of them had ever met. He was so smart, in fact, that everyone wondered why he was teaching middle school when he could've had a much better job. Rumor was that he had taught at a famous university, but he'd accidentally killed a student during a failed time-travel experiment. Blew up half the classroom. Someone else heard he'd shot a man in Reno just to watch him die, but Tunes said that was a line from a country song, so none of them knew what to believe.

"You know, Mr. J," Brooke said after swallowing the last bite of her Snickers, "the whole 'sugar leads to hyperactivity in children' theory is wrong. Scientists disproved that years ago." She swigged the last of her Coke and smugly clunked the can down on her desk.

"True," Mr. J said. "The only question I have is, why didn't our science expert point that out?" He turned to face Theo, who was chewing an especially large bite of candy bar.

With everyone in the room staring at him, Theo tried to talk, but all the chocolate and Snickers stuffing muffled his words. Just as well. All he had to say was, "I don't know."

Brooke took Theo's faltering as an opportunity to deliver a kung fu deathblow. "In fact, experts say that there is no correlation between food and behavior. More likely, kids' hyperactivity results from the excitement caused by parties and holidays, when they get more sweets than usual. Hence the mistaken blame on sugar."

"Great answer, Brooke," Mr. J said. "Except I'm deducting three points for using the word 'hence.' That's too geeky even for us."

Brooke snorted. Snorting was her major form of expression. Theo had started numbering her snorts the way he numbered his shrugs. Her Number 7 meant: "You are too stupid to say anything to me that I would ever want to hear." Snort Number 3 meant: "If you continue to breathe the same air as me, you will wake up one morning in a burlap bag in the middle of an African desert." They were all pretty much variations of those two.

Mr. J stood in front of Theo. He wasn't much taller standing than Theo was sitting. He had long brown hair that he wore pulled back into a thick braid, like rope on a whaling ship. He black jeans hung loose around his thin legs. He always wore a white (well, whitish) shirt that was so wrinkled it looked like he'd slept in it. For a month. Under a bridge.

He looked down at Theo's chessboard and smiled. "You're getting better."

"Thanks," Theo said, genuinely pleased. He felt a small chill at the back of his neck. His mouth went slightly dry. Maybe this time . . . The excitement made him shift uncomfortably in the small desk.

"By the way, Theo," Mr. J said, "what is Maggot Debridement Therapy?"

Theo felt all the blood rush from his head like panicky residents abandoning a burning building. "I think it's . . . uh . . . well, maggots are . . . uh—"

Brooke interrupted. Somehow, she managed to snort out the words. "Maggot Debridement Therapy is when live disinfected maggots—a.k.a. fly larvae—are dropped into an infected open wound, because they eat the dead skin cells as well as the bacteria."

"I concur," said Tunes.

"Shut up," Brooke said, and Tunes ducked his head as if she'd hurled the words at him. "Anyway, they discovered this on the battlefield. Doctors noticed that wounded soldiers with maggots in their wounds healed faster than soldiers without maggots. Now we have antibiotics, but because so many microbes are becoming resistant to them, lots of major modern hospitals around the world are using maggots. Even here in the U.S."

"No way," Daryl said, his face scrunched in disgust. "That's gross."

"About eight hundred medical centers in the U.S. use them," Brooke said.

Mr. J nodded in approval and Brooke went back to studying her chessboard. "That's the kind of thinking we're going to need to beat Lansing. As Shakespeare has Henry V saying:

"In peace there's nothing so becomes a man
    As modest stillness and humility;

But when the blast of war blows in our ears,
Then imitate the action of the tiger:
Stiffen the sinews, summon up the blood."

He practically shouted "summon up the blood," and everyone—even Brooke—jumped a little in their seats. For a few seconds, as his heart beat wildly in his chest, Theo could see on their faces that they each believed they might just beat Lansing.

"By the way, Theo," Mr. J said softly, nudging his queen two spaces, "checkmate in four moves."

IN the cafeteria, everyone Theo passed gave him a weird look. Some looked mildly amused, as if watching an Internet video of a dog walking on its hind legs carrying a tray. Most just looked surprised, as if this was the first time they realized he went to their school. One kid punched the air and then gave him a thumbs-up.

"How did word about the fight get out so fast?" Theo asked. "I just told you guys."

Daryl took a bite from his hamburger while they walked. "I texted Wolfman while Mr. J was wiping up the chessboard with your carcass."

"What'd you tell him?"

"That you were in a bare-knuckle brawl in the park. I might've mentioned that an ambulance was called. Oh, and that you threw rocks at a Hell's Angels biker who was hitting on your girlfriend. Admittedly, I embellished a little to hook the reader."

Theo spun, his carton of milk and plate of pizza almost sliding off his tray. "I didn't want the whole school to know!"

"Then why'd you tell us? You know none of us can keep our mouth shut."

Thing was, Daryl was right. Why had he told them—notorious blabbermouths—if he'd wanted it to remain a secret? Deep down, did he want everyone to know?

Theo shook off that question and walked away. "Never mind," he said. "Just never mind."

He walked outside to the metal picnic tables.

Daryl and Tunes hurried off in a different direction to join their buddies at the World of Warcraft table. They would spend the rest of the lunch break discussing their online strategies against the Horde.

Brian followed Theo to an empty table at the edge of the eating area. No one ever sat there because it was just outside the shade and the metal got as hot as a frying pan. But it was private.

They plopped their trays down opposite each other. Brian started right in. "What's up with you, dude?"

"Nothing. I told you what happened. It wasn't a big deal."

"I'm not talking about the fight. I'm talking about Mr. J's practice session. Maggot Debridement Therapy, Theo! It has 'maggot' in the title. We joked about it when we first read that article in the Aca-lympics study material. Last year you knew all about it."

It was true. Theo remembered now. Why hadn't he remembered in the classroom?

"What's going on with you? You grew a few inches and it stretched your brain out of shape?"

"I'm just . . . distracted. Suddenly Gavin's got talent and—"

"I hate to admit it, man, but he really is good."

Not what Theo wanted to hear. He continued his sentence. "—and I found out Friday night that my dad has secretly joined some online dating service."

"Whoa, Marcus is on the prowl?" Brian laughed. "'Imitate the action of the tiger: Stiffen the sinews, summon up the blood.'"

Theo chuckled. Brian could always make him laugh, even when he was feeling low.

"Has he actually gone out with any women yet?" Brian asked.

"No, he just joined."

"How'd you find out so fast?"

Theo told him about sneaking downstairs and breaking into the computer.

Brian stared with his mouth open. "Who are you, dude?"

Theo shrugged. "I've been asking myself that a lot lately."

They ate in silence for a while. Brian gobbled down two pieces of pizza, a bottle of water, and a chocolate cookie. Then he ate Theo's cookie. "Have you considered quitting basketball? Maybe that's the cause of all this chaos in your life. It's messing with your mind."

"It's not basketball. Basketball is just a game."

"No, it's not. It's a cult. Every sport at school is a cult. A bunch of kids playing because"—he peeled a finger for each reason—"one, their parents want to raise a sports hero so they can attend all the games and prove to everyone else what great parents they are."

"That's not my dad."

Brian shrugged, as if not wanting to debate it yet. "Okay. Two, because the players want everyone to notice them and think they are massively cool."

"Does that sound like me?"

"Three, because they're poor and a sports scholarship is their only hope of attending college. There are only about five kids at this whole school who qualify as poor, and none of them is on a sports team here."

Theo snorted. (Brooke would have appreciated that.) "What about just for the fun of playing the game?"

"You hadn't even heard of the game until a couple months ago, when Coach Mandrake asked you to join the team."

"I had heard of basketball. I'd even played in that summer camp, remember? We both did."

"That was for one week when we were eight and our parents still hoped we'd be normal kids instead of nerds."

True. Every summer their parents had rotated them among various sports camps: basketball, baseball, soccer, volleyball, football—even tennis. Theo and Brian had hated those camps, even though the coaches had been nice about the fact that sports balls were like kryptonite to the boys: when holding one, they lost all coordination and control over their bodies.

Eventually, they were sent to science camp to build robots and rockets. They'd loved it.

Just then, Chris Richards, the usually silent captain of the basketball team, walked by with his empty tray. "See ya at practice," he said, and kept walking.

When Chris was gone, Brian laughed. "So let me get this straight. *You* will be at practice and *Chris* will be at practice, ergo he will indeed see you there. Wow, what a breaking news bulletin."

Theo watched Chris walk away. Had he meant anything by that comment? Theo was in a couple of classes with other members of the basketball team, yet none had ever spoken to him about basketball. It was as if they were pretending he wasn't really on the team. Was Chris just being a friendly teammate, or was it some kind of threat because of what Coach had said about building the team around Theo? Were they going to "see" him at practice, but somehow mess him up? "Accidentally" break an arm or leg on the court?

"Maybe he's been watching too much *Avatar.* 'I seeee you.'" Brian said it slowly and creepily, the way they did in the movie.

Or maybe, Theo thought, they were okay with him now

because he had been in a fight. Or because he had been playing streetball, trying to improve. Maybe things were changing. For the better.

"I seeeee you, Theo. Do you seeeee me? Do you seeee my pizza?"

Three girls whispered to one another as they walked by Theo and Brian's table. But one of the girls, Sissy Chen, smiled at Theo. Theo's mouth went so dry he had to stop chewing. Sissy was very pretty and smart, and Theo had noticed her several times before. He'd even tried to work up the courage to talk to her in algebra, but he never did.

The girls moved on quickly, still whispering and giggling, and Sissy didn't look back. But her smile had been real. So real he felt he could wrap it in a napkin, put it in his pocket, and feel it there all day.

Brian groaned and raised four fingers. "Fourth reason guys join sports teams: girls."

"I didn't join because of girls."

"No? Then why did you join?"

"I don't know. I really don't. I think I joined because I was asked. I'd never been asked before, and it felt good."

"Okay, now you can check it off your bucket list and move on. You can quit, you know."

"I know. I just . . ." Theo watched the kids drifting back to classes. "I just don't want to. I kinda like it, Brian. It's hard to explain."

"Is it? Or maybe you just—"

Suddenly a familiar voice interrupted them. "So, what are we discussing, boys?"

Theo spun around.

Crazy Girl.

"YOU'RE Crazy Girl!" Brian burst out. His eyes widened as if he were staring at the slasher in a hockey mask from a horror film. He actually leaned away from her.

She laughed. "Is that what Sasquatch calls me?"

Brian nodded.

Theo sighed. In the presence of a girl, Brian was powerless. All he could do was tell the truth.

She shrugged. "I've been called worse."

"I bet you have," Theo muttered.

"But most people call me by my name. Which is Rain Kadinski." She offered her hand and Brian reluctantly shook it.

"Brian Horowitz." Brian looked her over as he shook: black leather Doc Martens boots that laced to her knees. Purple-and-black-striped tights. Denim shorts. White T-shirt with the word LESS printed on the front in tiny black letters.

"Your name is Rain?" Theo asked.

"Yup. My parents wanted to ruin my life from day one. Every time I introduce myself, I have to give an explanation.

Yes, it's my real name. Yes, I get teased. No, I don't want to be a weather forecaster. No, my parents aren't hippies. Just once I'd appreciate it if someone said, 'Pleased to meet you, Rain,' and that was that. Can you imagine if I added up all the minutes of explanation throughout my lifetime? I've wasted *years* talking about my name. Like right now, for example." She picked up Theo's half-eaten pizza, plucked off the pepperonis, and took a huge bite. "Jeez, I'm starving. I missed lunch." She tossed the remaining crust back onto his plate. "Thanks."

"What are you doing here?" Theo asked.

"Chillin' with my new buds." She laughed again, drank some of Brian's milk.

Brian recoiled as if she'd licked a toilet. When she put the milk back on his tray, he said, "That's all right. You can finish it."

She did.

Brian and Theo exchanged looks that said: "Who does that? Who eats a stranger's pizza? Drinks his milk?"

"What are you doing at our school?" Theo demanded, like a cop who's just caught a burglar and wants to know where the stolen loot is hidden.

"Attending classes, dude. I go here, too. Have been for a month. That's why I was at your basketball game yesterday. I just got the bleachers mixed up and sat on the opposing team's side."

"You go here?" Theo said. "How come I haven't seen you before?"

"For one, we're not in any of the same classes. For another, you're not very observant. But that's typical for a resident of Walla-Walla Land."

"Walla-Walla Land?" Brian asked.

"Don't encourage her, Brian. Let's go." Theo started to get up, but Brian didn't, apparently under Crazy Girl/ Rain's spell.

"Walla-walla," she explained, "is what they call the background noise in movies. You know, when the main characters are having dinner and discussing their relationship, but you can still hear the other diners in the background muttering and clanging their silverware. That background noise is called walla-walla. I have a cousin who's a film major at UCLA."

"What's that got to do with me?" Theo asked.

"That's where you live, isn't it? Both of you? In the background? A dim noise that can't quite be identified?"

An uncomfortable silence settled in.

"You're kind of mean," Brian finally said.

"I'm not being mean. I live there, too. I recognize my own kind. Like dogs, only without the awkward sniffing."

"Hey, Theo," Tunes called from the WOW table. "Is this right?" He played the piano app on his phone. It was Gavin's song. Other students turned to listen.

"Why are you playing that?" Theo snapped.

"Because it's a cool tune. I think I remember most of it." He tapped out the melody and sang a few lyrics. Students at other tables nodded, impressed. When he was done, he called, "Is that right?"

Theo turned away. "I don't know, and I don't care."

"Can I borrow the CD from your backpack so I can burn a copy?"

"No!" Theo said. "I told you, it's supposed to be private. He doesn't want other people listening to it."

"Too late," one of his WOW buddies said with a chuckle.

"Sorry, man," Tunes said, and put his phone away.

Everyone returned to what they were doing as if nothing had happened. Theo thought everything in middle school was like that. Students went through the day like pets on a leash. When something shiny or loud caught their attention, they all looked and barked for a few seconds, then continued walking until they passed the next shiny or loud thing.

"This day sucks," Theo muttered.

"It's about to get suckier," Brian said. "Bogie at three o'clock!"

Theo and Rain turned to see Brooke approaching with another girl beside her. The other girl was a seventh grader, Constance Rodriguez, who was an alternate on the Brain Train team. The alternates trained at a separate time, and then the two teams had a mock showdown before official matches as a way to prep the first team. The first team always beat the alternate team. Theo had been on the alternate team for two years. Last year he and Constance were on it together. Constance was very smart.

"Don't walk too close to her, Constance," Brian whispered to Theo, "you'll burst into flames."

Theo laughed.

"What's so funny?" Brooke said. "Never mind, I'm sure it was some sort of adolescent male insult directed at me."

Theo and Brian looked away.

Brooke checked out Rain as if she were a broken toy she'd received for Christmas. One dipped in dog poop. Then she ignored her and focused on Theo. "After your pathetic performance today, I proposed to Mr. J that we send you down as an alternate and bring Constance up to replace you."

"*What?!*" Brian hollered. Several students still eating lunch turned to look. "You can't do that!"

"Can. Did."

"But Theo is one of the best members of the team."

"Was. Isn't. Notice the verb tense change?"

Theo didn't know what to say. It had never occurred to him that even Brooke would ever do something as terrible as this to him. "What did Mr. J say?" he finally asked.

"He didn't say yes. But he didn't say no." She almost smiled. "He said it was an interesting suggestion and he would take it under advisement."

Theo was even more shocked. He would have expected Mr. J to kick her out of his office, maybe even off the team, for making such an underhanded suggestion. Theo knew

Mr. J was a teacher and all, but he thought they were sort of friends. As much as you could be with a teacher.

"Dude," Brian said to Brooke, "you are like some kind of Evil Queen or Wicked Witch. Seriously."

Brooke snorted. Theo recognized it as Snort Number 16: "Whatever you said isn't worth listening to because you are beneath my notice."

Theo considered Constance. They'd been friendly when they were both alternates. She'd once told him about her dog getting hit by a car, and he'd been sympathetic. Now Constance seemed to be in a state of shock rather than excitement. Theo realized that was because she hadn't known what Brooke had done. Brooke had probably told Constance to follow her to Theo's table, and she had done so because, well, people did what Brooke told them to do.

"Anyway," Brooke said, "I don't like going behind anyone's back, so I'm telling you to your face. It's not personal. Just what's best for the team." She looked right at Theo, and he could see that there was no anger or spite in her eyes. She believed what she was saying. "You're holding us back, Theo."

Brooke walked away, and Constance hurried behind her, trying to catch up. Constance glanced over her shoulder at Theo and mouthed, "Sorry." But, of course, that wouldn't stop her from replacing him.

"Man, this stinks!" Brian said. "We should go talk to Mr. J."

"Why?" Rain asked. Was she actually eating the cookie crumbs from Brian's tray?

"Because she's trying to get me kicked off the team," Theo said, "that's why."

"Is she wrong?" She licked her fingers of the last crumbs.

"What?" Brian asked, shocked by the question.

"Is she wrong about Theo's performance on the team? Has he been slacking off? Is he pulling the team down?"

Theo and Brian looked at each other.

"That's not the point!" Brian snapped. "The point is we're friends, and you don't ditch a friend like that. I bet Daryl and Tunes will back us up. If Theo goes, we'll all quit."

Rain wagged her head back and forth like she was weighing both sides. "That's noble and all, but if Theo is such a good friend, shouldn't he be pulling his weight? Isn't that his duty as a friend to the rest of you?"

"He's also got basketball practice," Brian said.

"Maybe he can't do both."

Brian started to answer, then hesitated. Brian was loyal, Theo knew, but he was also smart. Good arguments were good arguments and he couldn't deny them.

Theo stood up, grabbed his tray, and started walking away. Brian followed. "You wouldn't understand friendship," Theo said to Rain without turning, "because you don't have any friends."

"Maybe," she replied. "But am I wrong about you?"

"CATCH the freakin' *ball*, Theo!"

"Dribble toward the basket, Theo! *Toward!*"

"Don't shoot! Pass it, dude! Pass it *now!*"

"Bounce-pass, Theo! *Bounce-pass!*"

Theo's teammates were hollering at him the way they would at a stray dog who was running off with their backpacks. He tried to follow their advice, but it was just too hard to do everything at once. And everything he did do was wrong.

Whatever goodwill he'd earned from the rumors of his playing at the park and standing up to Motorcycle Guy had been erased by his stumbling around the court today like a three-legged rabbit caught in a cattle stampede. As far as his teammates were concerned, he was back to square one.

Square one sucked!

Practice that day had started with so much hope.

As the team was dressing in the locker room, a couple guys who'd never even spoken to Theo off court had nodded hello. One kid had called him "slugger" in a nonsarcastic way. Roger and Sinjin ignored him, but that meant they didn't insult him, so this was progress.

"Listen up, men!" Coach shouted from his office. "Everybody in here on the double. Hustle it up!"

The players hurried into his office. Coach Mandrake sat behind his messy desk, waving everyone in. "C'mon, c'mon. There's plenty of room."

The boys crowded closer to look at his computer screen.

Theo noticed three Starbucks coffee cups on the desk. Two had been there so long that they had begun to leak coffee onto the papers beneath them. Most of the papers on the desk had old coffee rings on them. Coach didn't seem to care.

"I want to show you boys something," Coach said.

He clicked on a YouTube video.

The boys watched the screen as a high school basketball team filed into a gym. Among them was a black boy who towered so far above his teammates that they all looked like toddlers.

"That's Mamadou N'Diaye," Coach said.

"Yeah, I've heard of him," Roger said. "He's playing at that Christian high school in Huntington Beach. He's like nine feet tall or something."

"Seven feet five inches," Coach said. "He's only seventeen, but considered the tallest high school player in the world. Watch what they do."

The clip showed the team running the same play over and over. They'd throw Mamadou the ball, he'd turn around, take one step, and dunk it through the hoop. Sometimes another player would shoot. If he missed, Mamadou would grab the rebound, turn, and dunk.

"Dude," Sami Russell whispered in awe. Sami was the smallest guy on the team, but also the fastest.

"Yeah." Thomas Farley nodded. Thomas was the team's best free throw shooter.

"Catch, turn, drop-step, dunk," Coach said. "That's their strategy, and that's basically going to be ours."

Everyone looked at Theo.

Theo's stomach twisted like a wet rag being wrung.

"Coach," Theo said, "first, that guy's almost a foot taller than me. Second, I can't dunk."

"A layup is as good as a dunk, Theo."

"He can't do a layup either," Roger said.

A few boys murmured agreement.

Coach waved dismissively. "I'm not saying we don't have some work to do. But we have to take advantage of what we have. Besides, we don't need Theo to make all the shots. He needs to just make enough that the other side double-teams him. That will leave one of our guys open, and Theo can pass the ball to him for a free shot." Coach stood up. "Now get out on the court and give me a couple laps. Then we start running our new plays. Today is the start of a whole new dynasty for the Ravens."

"Ravens!" a couple guys hollered enthusiastically as they ran out to the gym.

"Theo," Coach said as the other boys hustled off.

Theo stopped.

Coach waited until the others were gone. He stared at Theo with a serious expression. "You can do this, Theo."

Theo nodded. "Right."

"You have to believe that, son."

Theo kept nodding. "Right. I do."

But, of course, he didn't believe it. Any more than he believed in the Easter Bunny or Looks-Don't-Matter-It's-What's-Inside-That-Counts.

Practice proved him right.

He chest-passed when he should have bounce-passed. Result: interception.

He pivoted on the wrong foot. Result: traveling.

He cleared out players with his left hand while reaching for the lob pass with his right hand. Result: foul.

He lowered his shoulder into the defender when moving toward the basket. Result: foul.

He reached in to swat at the ball while the offense backed into him. Result: foul.

When trying to block a shot, he fell forward into the shooter. Result: foul.

After forty minutes, Coach blew the whistle for a team huddle.

Theo shuffled in exhausted, sweat running down his face.

"Coach," Roger said with frustration, "he's gonna foul out of every game before we get to use your strategy."

"Dude," Sami said to Theo, "you gotta stop hacking. Players are supposed to hack you and foul out, not the other way around."

"Sorry," Theo said.

Chris Richards spoke. It was so rare an occurrence that the other boys parted to allow his words to be heard. "Use your hips to keep him in place," Chris said. "Don't even try for the ball. One of us will swing around and pressure him to force a bad pass or weak shot. Then you've got position. You can box him out and snag the rebound."

"Right, Chris," Coach said. "That's exactly right."

The boys all nodded in agreement, like parishioners at Theo's grandma's church. Theo half expected to hear an "Amen!" or "Hallelujah!"

Coach waved them all in closer. "Look, you all did fine today. Theo, you just tried a little too hard, tried to force things. But as we keep practicing the plays, you'll relax, get more comfortable. Let's give it a week and see where we stand then. If it's not working, we'll make some changes." Coach rubbed his hands together enthusiastically as the boys moved toward the locker room. "It's a process, boys. A process."

Process, Theo thought. Another word for square one.

LATER that afternoon, Brian and Theo were on the park swings, watching the pickup games while eating Butterfingers and drinking Gatorade.

"You're not going down there again, are you?" Brian asked, glancing at the basketball courts.

Theo shrugged. "I don't know. The team is counting on me. Actually, they're counting on me to keep screwing up, and I don't want them to be right." He didn't mention that Coach had said they'd give the new plan a week and then "make some changes." Translation: kick Theo off the team.

"Remember my motto: no good comes from physical activity. Especially in a public place."

Theo laughed. "Your two greatest fears: exercise and sweaty strangers."

"Add crappy drinks to that list." Brian frowned at his bottle. "Since when do we drink Gatorade? It seems to counter the whole point of eating candy bars. Candy bars aren't just about having a sweet treat; they're also about defying the smug health tips of our parents and teachers.

We're shaking our fists at society, rebelling against their sensible lessons. Each bite of a Butterfinger is like a Boston Tea Party, and we're throwing over crates of tea that symbolize our teenage repression. Candy fuels the teen revolution!"

Theo looked at him. "Is it any wonder our only friends are Daryl and Tunes?"

"Point taken," Brian said, biting into his candy bar.

They watched the games in silence. Well, as silent as it could be with Brian munching and slurping.

From up here, Theo noticed how smoothly the kids moved around the court. Like they were ice-skating. Nothing like the way he moved on his long, stupid legs. Sometimes, he felt as if his body were recovering from a painful accident rather than just adjusting to a growth spurt.

"We have other friends," Brian suddenly said. While Theo had been thinking about having stilts for legs, Brian had been obsessing over Theo's comment about friends.

"Like who?"

Brian thought. "Brooke talked to us today. That's progress."

"She didn't talk to *us*. She threatened *me*."

"That's progress. First threats, then an invitation to her cool house."

Theo did a perfect imitation of Brooke's snort and they both laughed.

"Okay," Brian continued, "what about Rain? She seems nice. And she's a girl. Not like Brooke, who is eighty-six percent cyborg."

"Rain is not our friend. She's . . ." Theo struggled to find the words.

"Hygienically challenged? Did you see her eat food we'd already had our diseased mouths on?"

"My mouth isn't diseased."

"Dude, everyone's mouth is diseased. The adult mouth contains five hundred to a thousand different types of bacteria. Even a cleanliness freak like me, who brushes after every meal and carries a secret stash of Scope, has one thousand to a hundred thousand bacteria living on each tooth surface. If I ignored my dental hygiene altogether, like Marty Fenster in social studies, I'd have a hundred million to one billion bacteria on each tooth. Each tooth! Rain ate food our teeth touched!" Brian was so upset he had to take a big swig of Gatorade to calm himself.

"What about the two micrograms of rat poop and hairs the government allows in candy bars?"

Brian studied his Butterfinger a moment, then took a big bite. "Acceptable risk considering the reward." His face brightened. "Hey, maybe that's what Rain is?"

"Rat poop?"

"No, an acceptable risk considering the reward. After all, she's a girl. She talked to us without needing to copy our homework or borrow anything. Just to talk. That's huge, dude."

Girls. It seemed as if, since they turned thirteen, more and more of their conversations ended up being about girls. They'd start out talking about the cool animation in a new Batman video game and end up talking about how hot Catwoman was. Or they'd be discussing an awesome scene from a zombie movie in which some greasy undead guy is ripping out someone's gooey insides, and suddenly they were arguing about whether, if your girlfriend was turned into a zombie, you'd be able to cut off her head. And now their conversation about mouth bacteria had drifted into talking about Rain.

Theo had a philosophy about girls (yes, even though he'd never had a girlfriend). According to him, there were two types: Desert Girls, and Dessert Girls. Desert Girls were the kind you could be trapped with on a desert island and they wouldn't complain about the bugs or the food or not having the Internet. They would help build the boat that you'd need to escape, and talk cheerfully the whole time about what a great adventure this was. Dessert Girls, on the other hand, were the kind who stood at dessert buffets pointing out the different things they would looove to eat but couldn't because of the calories. They would gossip about the other girls who *did* take dessert and how they shouldn't because they'd bloat up. They never noticed anything or anyone but themselves and whatever it was they wanted. Which, in this case, was dessert.

Rain definitely wasn't a Dessert Girl, but he couldn't imagine being trapped on a desert island with her either.

She'd probably build the boat by herself. And eat all their pineapples and coconuts. And sail away without him.

"You know," Brian said, "we're thirteen. We really should be going out with girls. I don't necessarily mean on a *date*, but maybe hanging around with them. Talking to them. Working up to being alone with one, like at a movie. Alone in a crowd. You know what I mean. If we start now, we might have a date by senior prom."

"We're too young."

"Or too chicken."

Theo nodded. "Yeah, there's that."

Theo tried to imagine himself on a date with Sissy. Burgers and shakes at Red Robin. A movie. Something not too violent, but no romantic comedies either. Something beige. Something out of an Archie comic book.

Theo's dad had offered to drive him to the multiplex and pick him up again if he ever wanted to meet a girl there. Thankfully, he hadn't pushed it any further. Theo would act when he was good and ready. Problem was, he'd been feeling good and ready for a while now, and he'd done nothing about it.

"Who would you ask out?" Brian asked. He took a last swig of Gatorade and sat staring at the three kids on the court playing horse.

"Sissy Chen. You?"

Brian shrugged. "So many to choose from." It came out in a sad, defeated voice.

"Dude, you're smart and funny and the coolest guy I

know. There are plenty of girls at school who would hang out with you."

"I think I heard that line in an old John Hughes movie."

"In all the John Hughes movies. That's why I remembered it."

They laughed.

"See? That's all I want," Brian said. "A girl who would know what I'm talking about when I mention John Hughes movies. Especially *Breakfast Club*." He took another bite of candy. "Maybe I want Molly Ringwald."

"She's probably older than your mother by now."

Brian sighed. "Man, thirteen sucks. No wonder it's an unlucky number."

"I know. Suddenly everyone's piling on all this new responsibility, but without any respect. When you want to do something new, they say, 'You're only thirteen.' But when they want you to do more work, they say, 'You're thirteen now, not a kid.'"

"Hey, try going through all that while at the same time learning Hebrew."

"At least you got an awesome bar mitzvah party out of it."

"True. I got like a thousand bucks in gift cards. Got my new laptop with them."

Laptop. That made Theo think about how he had snuck down to spy on his dad's computer.

Theo suddenly realized he was feeling—not guilty, surprisingly—but angry. Yet he didn't know about what exactly. "You know what bugs me most? When you're thirteen, parents still want to see you as innocent, but I don't feel so innocent. They sigh when you take down the Harry Potter posters and put up Fall Out Boy and the Killers. They wince when you don't want to make an ice-cream run like you used to. And you feel so guilty, because everything you do or don't do seems to hurt them."

"I told my dad I didn't want to watch *America's Funniest Home Videos* anymore and he actually got tears in his eyes."

"That's what I mean. They want us to stay cute and cuddly, like a kitten. But sometimes I feel mean and selfish. Sometimes I don't care about the homeless or the baby seals or starving children in Africa. Or even that I hurt his feelings because I don't want to listen to Motown classics. Sometimes I just feel . . ."

"Sexy?"

Theo laughed. "Maybe, I don't know. What I do know is that I'm not the kid that people see when they look at me. Even my dad. It's like they think that if you feed vegetarian kibble to a dog all his life, when a piece of steak falls on the floor, he won't go for it. But he will. He'll gobble it right up and sniff around for more. Because he's a dog, and that's what dogs do."

"Yeah, but it'll probably give him diarrhea."

"That's my point. Adults keep telling us that everything we want will give us diarrhea. Girls will give us STDs. Video games will make us violent. Rock music is bad for our hearing."

"My uncle used to follow Phish around to all their concerts and now he has two hearing aids, so they were right about that one."

Theo frowned at Brian. "Dude, you suck at these talks."

He shrugged. "Plus, all this talk of steak has made me hungry." He wrestled his body out of the small swing. "Time to head home. You coming?"

Theo kept his eyes on the boys shooting baskets. "I'll catch you later."

"Suit yourself," said Brian. "Just don't take any more punches, okay?"

"I'll try," said Theo, in all seriousness. Because one of the three guys on the nearest court was Asian Kid. The one who'd punched him Friday.

THEO avoided the court Asian Kid was using. Instead, he went to the court farthest away, where some sixth and seventh graders were playing. They were happy to have him, not because he was better than they were (he was average), but because he was older and still wanted to play with them.

"We're just fooling around," Skinny Neck said. He nodded toward Jeremy and the others. "We're not that intense."

"That's cool," Theo said.

Skinny Neck was right. They weren't intense. In fact, they were so relaxed that no one seemed to take the game seriously. They joked around a lot, took impossible trick shots, and constantly chatted during play. When someone missed a shot, they made fun of him, and the object of the ridicule would also laugh.

Theo hated it.

This was no way for him to improve his game. Even though some of the players were actually better than he was, no one was really trying. No one cared about the score. They were just a bunch of friends playing an endless game that would last their entire childhood.

Part of Theo understood that. Admired that.

Yet he still hated it.

He wanted to become better, and they weren't cooperating with his plan. Even when he scored on someone, the kid would just smile and say, "Good shot." They said it after anyone made a basket, so it didn't really mean anything.

After the third game ended, they all took a break. Theo had filled his Gatorade bottle with water from the fountain. He drank from it while the other boys horsed around, joking and talking about some trouble their friends had gotten into at school. The only difference between when they were playing and now was that no one was dribbling a ball.

Theo was deciding whether or not to leave when he suddenly saw Asian Kid coming toward him. Maybe he's just going to use the bathrooms up the hill, he thought. Or the drinking fountain.

But Jeremy was staring right at him. When he got within a few feet of Theo, he brought his closed fist up.

"Hey, man," Jeremy said. "Sorry about yesterday. My bad." He extended his fist.

Theo fist-bumped him. Jeremy nodded, turned, and walked back to his pals.

And that was that. Apology. Fist bump. All is forgiven. Theo smiled. Cool.

Theo played one more game with the Happy Jokesters and decided to leave. Playing these guys wouldn't help him, yet he wasn't good enough to play with Jeremy and the others, which would make him better. He needed to figure this out. He had just started up the hill when he saw R. J. Thompson walking down toward the courts.

R.J. was the star athlete of the high school where Theo would be going next year. R.J. was only a junior, but he was the leading scorer on the football, basketball, and volleyball teams. R.J. was tall (though not as tall as Theo), lean, muscular—and black. Out of 689 students at the high school, there were 36 black students. And every one of those 689 knew who R.J. was.

He was walking with two white kids, both seniors whom Theo recognized because others were always pointing them out at McDonald's or Best Buy, as if they couldn't believe these gods walked among the normal people. R.J. and his friends were talking and laughing like they knew that no matter what they did, it was cool, no matter what they said, it was funny.

Theo had never spoken to R.J.—they'd never even met—but as they passed now, they both looked at each other and half nodded, like two undercover cops trying not to blow each other's cover.

As they neared the basketball court where Jeremy and his friends were, the players all greeted them enthusiastically as if to say, "Finally, we can play some *real* ball."

For a moment, Theo wondered if R.J.'s life was what his dad had in mind for him. Did he envision Theo swaggering into rooms like a gunslinger? Theo sighed and walked on. He thought about his dad, Mr. J, Coach, and R.J. until his phone buzzed to tell him he had a text message.

Caller Unknown: *Really? Ur playing with little kids now? What would Dr. J say?*

Crazy Girl/Rain. Theo looked around. Where was she?

Theo: *How did u get my number?*

Caller Unknown: *Please. My dog could hack ur number and she only has 3 legs.*

Theo: *What happened to the other leg? U eat it?*

Caller Unknown: *Hahaha. But not as funny as u at practice today.*

She'd seen him at practice. How? Coach didn't allow spectators. Where had she been hiding?

Theo saw the time on his phone and realized he had to hurry home before he was late for dinner. He texted as he jogged.

Theo: *Why r u following me?*

There was no answer. Maybe she was home already and her mom had her doing chores.

Then, Caller Unknown: *U need a personal trainer, dude. And fast.*

Theo: *Why do u care?*

Again, no response. Theo kept staring at the screen. He had finally started to type another message when a voice made him lift his head.

"Where is she?" Motorcycle Guy demanded, standing in front of Theo with his red-flame helmet tucked under one arm. He leaned forward until his face was within inches of Theo's and yelled, "Where's Rain?"

WHERE'S Rain?

If this were a Bruce Willis *Die Hard* movie, Theo would have had a funny comeback line to put Motorpsycho—his new nickname for the guy—in his place.

Where's Rain? Have you checked the rain forest, pal?

Where's Rain? You go straight up about five thousand feet and turn left at the cumulonimbus cloud on the corner.

Where's Rain? Get naked, swing a dead chicken over your head, and chant. Then you'll have rain.

But Theo didn't have a team of million-dollar Hollywood writers coming up with witty hero dialogue. So, with the guy screaming in his face, all Theo could come up with was, "I dunno."

Motorpsycho stared without expression. It was getting dark out, and his long black hair and black leather outfit made his body seem to disappear. His angry face floated in front of Theo like a severed head.

"You think this is a joke?" Motorpsycho asked. His harsh accent came from the back of the throat and picked up a lot of phlegm before the actual words came gargling out. "Do you?"

"No," Theo said. He most certainly did not think this was a joke, as the trembling in his legs proved. "It's just that I don't really know her. I only met her a few days ago."

"And yet you came running to assist her. Big hero."

Motorpsycho was about six feet tall—shorter than Theo—but even in the darkness, his extra thirty pounds of muscle were an obvious presence. One thing kept running through Theo's mind: Don't hit me. Don't hit me. Don't hit me.

Well, two things.

Don't kill me. Don't kill me. Don't kill me.

"Is that not true?" Motorpsycho insisted. "Aren't you a big hero?"

Theo shrugged. "Not really. I wasn't thinking."

Was that as lame and cowardly as it sounded? Theo lowered his head in shame.

"Did she tell you where she is staying?" Motorpsycho asked. Suddenly his voice was softer, almost gentle, like they were now pals. Facebook friends liking each other's vacation photos and sharing videos that made fun of Justin Bieber.

He poked Theo hard in the shoulder. "Well, did she?"

Theo shook his head.

Motorpsycho frowned. "Do you think we are fools? You kids always think everyone else is a fool."

"No, I don't think anyone's a fool," Theo said. "I really don't know what you're talking about. I just met her Friday. I only found out her name today. If you'd asked me yesterday, 'Where's Rain?,' I would've thought you were talking about actual rain."

Theo couldn't stop babbling. Through the sound of his own chattering voice, he remembered Motorpsycho saying "we" ("Do you think we are fools?"). Was there more than one of him?

A loud whistle, like someone calling his dog, cracked the night air.

Motorpsycho glanced over his shoulder toward some trees. Theo saw another figure half emerge from the shadows. Also dressed in black, but with the helmet on, the visor down, so Theo couldn't see the face.

Motorpsycho grabbed Theo's phone from his sweaty hand. Theo didn't protest. Motorpsycho did some quick thumb work on the keypad—much quicker than Theo had ever seen anyone work, even Debbie Seid, who on a dare texted the entire Declaration of Independence in less than two minutes. This kid knew something about computers.

Motorpsycho tossed the phone back to Theo. "Thank you, Theo Rollins, of 1256 Sandhurst Drive." He then rattled off Theo's e-mail address and phone number. "In case you decide you want to go home crying to your mommy and daddy, I'll know where to go to explain things to them. In the middle of the night. While they're sleeping."

"My dad's a cop," Theo blurted out defiantly.

Motorpsycho grinned as if Theo had told him his dad was a teddy bear. "Then by all means, tell him everything."

Theo didn't say anything. Why was this guy so smug? Why wasn't he afraid of the police?

"I've put a phone number in your phone. The moment you see her, call that number."

"I have no idea when, or if, I'll ever see her. Like I told you, I just met her a few days ago."

Motorpsycho glared at Theo and spoke through gritted teeth. "If you do not call me by Friday . . ." He didn't finish. He didn't have to. Theo could imagine the rest of the sentence. And in each variation, lots of pain was implied.

Motorpsycho ran up the slope toward his friend. They climbed onto their motorcycles and roared off into the night. It would have made a cool scene in a movie.

Except it isn't a movie. And he'll be coming after me.

Theo watched, waiting for his heart to stop somersaulting in his chest like a monkey being chased by a lion.

Crazy Girl.

Motorcycle Mafia.

Night assaults.

And all Theo wanted to do was play basketball.

"WHAT was the best thing that happened to you today?" Theo's dad asked.

They were eating his dad's default dinner: Knockwurst. Baked beans. Corn bread. Garbage Salad (a salad made from whatever they could scrounge up in the refrigerator). This was the menu whenever his dad was too tired to break out the cookbook. Which was every Monday. On Mondays he had to catch up on his cop-house paperwork.

Theo couldn't focus on his dad's question. During the whole walk home from the park, he'd been debating with himself about telling his dad about Motorpsycho. If this were a movie, the audience would be shouting, "Tell him, stupid!" But the stupid kid wouldn't, and then all these terrible things would happen that could have been avoided simply by telling his parents in the first place.

Moral of the story: Tell your parents everything.

That's the moral of every movie for kids.

But every kid in the world knows that's not the real world. Hollywood serves up neat and tidy lessons because that's what parents want. In the real world, parents can't solve every problem. They can't cure acne. Or stop you from acting like a spaz when a girl talks to you. Or help when kids make fun of your height. Or make sure you don't get kicked off the basketball team.

Or prevent your mom from getting killed.

Theo looked into his dad's kind eyes, and again a wave of shame drenched him. He had lied to his dad, snuck onto his computer, kept information from him. How could his dad ever trust him again? Worse, how could Theo ever trust himself? He was becoming the kind of kid he'd always tried to avoid at school.

Still, there were some things that Theo had to take care of himself. Like finding out what Rain had to do with Motorpsycho, and convincing both of them to leave him alone.

"How come every time I ask you that question lately, there's a long pause? Did something bad happen that you're not telling me?"

Theo shook his head and pretended to focus on buttering his corn bread. "Nothing good happened, that's all. Just the same boring crap every day. School, practice, homework. It's like being in the army." He looked up at his dad. "Anything happen to you that you're not telling me?"

His dad's expression remained blank. He was better than Theo at hiding his emotions. "Nope. Same ol' same ol'." He cut a piece of his knockwurst. "What's up with Brian?"

"Nothing."

"How's his dad doing? He had knee surgery recently, didn't he?"

"Yeah. He's fine, I guess. Limps a lot."

"How'd practice go?"

"Which one?"

His dad hesitated. Before basketball, he used to ask about Brain Train practice. Since basketball, he mostly asked about that. Another sign of how much he wanted Theo to be an athlete. Just like him.

"Both," his dad said.

"Well, Mr. J is considering kicking me off the Brain Train because I've fallen behind, and I think Coach might cut me from the basketball team because I stink up the court. So they both went about the same."

His dad didn't say anything. For a while, the only sound was the clinking of their forks against their plates.

Then Theo looked at his dad and said, "You ever think about dating again?"

Theo watched his dad's face for some sign of surprise. Nothing.

"Not really. Why?"

"No reason. It's been a while. I wondered if maybe you're lonely."

"You keep me too busy to get lonely," his dad joked.

"Come on, Dad. I know it's hard. You're still kind of young, I mean, for a dad."

Marcus remained quiet for a long time. When he did speak, his voice was low. "I miss your mom, and I will every day for the rest of my life. No matter what else happens, nothing will change that."

Theo didn't ask any more questions. Clearly his dad wasn't ready to mention the online dating. Well, they both had their secrets, which Theo assumed was part of being an adult. And, though part of him felt very adult and secret-agent-like, another part of him felt lonely and scared and very much like a kid.

"Can I be excused?" Theo asked, standing up from the dinner table. "I have a lot of homework."

"Yeah, sure," his dad said casually, but Theo could feel his concerned eyes watching him the entire time as he walked out of the kitchen and up the stairs.

In his room, Theo rushed through his homework. He knew he wasn't doing his usual conscientious job. He answered questions quickly and sloppily, but he was too distracted to care. He took out the Brain Train manual to study for tomorrow's practice session with Mr. J, knowing that if he failed to impress, Constance Rodriguez might replace him. After catching himself reading the same page about the earth's layers for the third time, though, he jumped off his bed, grabbed his basketball, and started practicing the triple-threat position that Coach had taught him. Ball down to his hip. Feet shoulder width apart. Knees bent. Weak hand on side of ball, strong hand on top. Pivot, pivot, pivot. Now you can pass, dribble, or shoot.

But he couldn't focus on that either, and he slammed the ball on his bed. All he could think about was Motorpsycho and his mysterious friend, Shadow Man. What did they want with Rain? What would they do to Theo if he didn't help them?

Finally, he pushed his papers aside and texted Rain. He'd stored her number as CG (for Crazy Girl).

Theo: *Ur motorcycle friend stopped me at park. He wanted to know where u are.*

Her response came almost instantly.

CG: *What did u tell him?*

Theo: *Nothing. What could I tell him?*

No response.

Theo: *Who is that guy? What does he want?*

Long pause.

CG: *My cousin.*

Theo: *Ur cousin doesn't know where you live?*

CG: *It's complicated.*

Theo: *What does he want?*

No response.

Theo waited a few minutes, then typed: *You still there?*

No response.

Theo plugged his phone into the charger, cleared his bed of the books, papers, and basketball, and crawled under the covers. He lay sleepless for an hour, tossing as if he were wrestling an invisible opponent.

His phone buzzed and he looked at the screen.

CG: *Good night.*

Theo: *We need to talk. He threatened me and my dad.*

CG: *Tomorrow.*

He texted back, demanding to know right now. But she never responded.

Then the house phone rang. Theo thought it might be Rain, so he quickly snatched up the extension on his desk. "Hello?"

A woman's voice. Not Rain's.

"Hello," she said, her voice pleasant. "May I speak to Marcus Rollins, please?"

"Who's calling?" Theo asked. His dad didn't want to be bothered by people selling time-shares or newspaper subscriptions.

Another extension clicked on, and Marcus's voice spoke: "It's okay, Theo. I've got it."

"Marcus?" she said. Her voice suddenly seemed lighter, happier.

"I've got it, Theo," his dad repeated, his voice firmer.

Theo hesitated. Who was this woman who was so happy to talk to his dad?

Finally, he said, "Okay," and hung up.

Theo sat on the edge of his bed for a few minutes, wondering about the woman on the phone. He didn't have time to formulate many theories, because his dad suddenly appeared in the doorway.

"Hey, T, I'm heading out for a little while. Be back late, so don't wait up." He tried to leave quickly, but Theo managed to fire off a question before he could escape.

"Where're you going?"

Marcus backed up until he was framed by the doorway. "Just meeting some friends."

"Who was that woman on the phone?"

"A friend."

"One of the friends you're going out to meet?"

Marcus looked at his watch. "Sorry, son, I don't have time for you break out the bright lights and lie detector. We'll continue the interrogation later."

He hurried away, his heavy footsteps thumping down the stairs as if he was taking two at a time. "Don't wait up!" he hollered from downstairs. "I mean it." Then the front door slammed shut and he was gone.

Two minutes later, Theo was logged onto his dad's computer and scrolling through Why Wait Mate, the dating site Marcus belonged to.

He clicked on "Favorites." There was one name: Miranda Sanjume. He clicked on it and a woman's photo and profile appeared. In the photo she stood in the middle of many rows of pineapples, holding a pineapple in each hand. Her profile said that her father was the foreman of a pineapple plantation in Hawaii. She lived in Newport Beach. She was a lawyer. Thirty-five. Never married.

Theo studied her face. Pretty. Half Asian, half something with darker skin. Filipino, maybe. Nice smile, not forced.

Theo clicked on "Photo Album" and a dozen photos opened. In one, she was crossing the finish line at a triathlon. In another, she was playing tennis. So, she was athletic. Another photo showed her in a business suit and carrying a briefcase as she entered the courthouse. She looked very serious and professional.

The last few photos showed her at music concerts. In one, she was sitting on the shoulders of an enormous Samoan man, both of her hands clenched in the classic rock-and-roll gesture: a fist with the index and pinkie fingers sticking up. The caption said: *With my brother, Turk, at AC/DC concert.* They were right next to the stage. In the second photo, she was once again next to the stage, this time reaching her hand out to Steven Tyler from Aerosmith, who was leaning down to touch it.

Theo wondered how she could afford such good seats at those concerts.

He shook his head. Not the point, Theo. Stay focused here.

He leaned back in his chair. Was she the one who had called? The one who had sent his dad rushing out of the house?

Theo felt frozen to the chair, unable to move or talk or breathe. Somehow, this felt like the beginning of something bad, like he'd just found out his dad robbed banks on the weekends. He could almost feel his world crumbling down around him.

BRIAN was late.

Brian was never late for lunch. Lunch was his reward for everything else he had to do at school. Sometimes he'd name his food after particularly annoying class incidents. Like his french fries would be called "Ms. Danbury's geography pop quiz," and his ice-cream sandwich would be called "Ms. Collins's Indian-camp diorama assignment." Then he'd eat them with a big smile, as if devouring his problems.

Theo was sitting at their usual lunch spot, anxiously looking all around. He'd just seen Brian at the school assembly, an intense hour about the horrors of bullying with a bunch of reformed bullies and formerly bullied recounting their experiences. One redheaded girl who had been cyber-bullied (a bunch of girls at her school had started a Facebook campaign to destroy her because she had red hair—they called her "Ginger-vitus") actually broke into tears and had to be escorted from the podium. That got most of the students' attention.

One "former" bully recounted all the different ways he'd bullied kids, from stealing their backpacks to smacking them in the back of the head with a textbook. He acted all sorry, but there was something in his voice that made Theo think he was kind of bragging about it, too.

Theo had used the time to work on his algebra homework.

He wasn't being insensitive; it was just that Orangetree Middle School didn't really have any serious bullying. Unlike in all the movies about schools, here there were no swirlies in the toilets, kids shoved into lockers, or lunch-money holdups (most kids' lunches were prepaid by computer). Occasionally someone might make fun of a kid's shoes or hair or breath, and sometimes an ethnic slur was bounced off a kid's head. Once a year someone punched someone else, but for the most part it was a peaceful school. Some kids complained that it was *too* peaceful. Not the kids who'd been punched, though.

Theo didn't deny the seriousness of bullying in other places. It was just that he was falling further and further behind in his studies, and he needed every spare minute to just keep afloat.

Theo had scanned the entire auditorium looking for Rain, but he didn't spot her. She said she went to the school, but he had yet to see her. She always managed to find him, though. He couldn't decide whether that was creepy or flattering.

Theo took a bite of his egg-salad sandwich while looking over the lunch crowd for Brian. And Rain.

He'd barely slept last night knowing that today she was going to explain everything about Motorpsycho. Crazily, Theo wondered if Motorpsycho had kidnapped Brian. Kidnapping or alien abduction were the only possible explanations for him being late for food.

Another thing kept him awake last night: waiting for his dad to come home. His dad had finally snuck up to his bedroom at about 12:30 A.M. His dad never stayed up that late. Even on weekends, when he and Theo would watch Netflix movies, his dad usually fell asleep by eleven at the latest.

This morning he'd acted like nothing had happened.

"How was your get-together last night?" Theo had asked.

"Good." His dad plopped a waffle on the table for Theo.

"Just good? You were out pretty late for just 'good.'"

Marcus didn't say anything. He shoved a piece of waffle into his mouth and shrugged.

Really? A shrug? Shrugging was Theo's specialty, not his dad's.

As Theo absentmindedly nibbled his sandwich while searching the lunch crowd, he was surprised by an unfamiliar voice.

"Hey, Theo," she said. Jackie Leonard. She went to Brian's temple, though Brian said she'd never talked to him there, except to tell him his fly was down. Her dad was an attorney for some former child star who now only got small parts on crime shows like *CSI* and *Law & Order*. Usually he was the killer.

"Oh, hey, Jackie," Theo said.

"My dad's taking a bunch of us to Disneyland next Saturday for my birthday. You wanna come?"

"Me?" That was all Theo could think to say. His first thought was that he was being punked. Jackie was very cute and bouncy in a Miranda Cosgrove way, and she had never talked to Theo before. He checked to see if his fly was down. Nope. So why now?

"Some of the other guys from the basketball team are going, and I thought you'd like to, too."

"Yeah, sure. That'd be great. Thanks." Theo thought his voice sounded pinched and wheezy, as if an elephant was standing on his chest.

"Great. Friend me on Facebook and I'll send you the details."

"Okay. Thanks. Thanks." He thanked her twice? How desperate was that?

Jackie walked off and was quickly joined by two other girls, because Jackie was the kind of girl who never had to go anywhere alone. Friends materialized out of thin air. If she ever got lost on a ski slope, she'd probably show up at the bottom with a couple of Yetis as her BFFs.

So why did she suddenly invite Theo to her party? Simply because he was on the basketball team? A warm sense of relief spread through his body. If that were true, then high school (which he had been secretly dreading for the past two years) would be easy. He would be popular, and not just the kid that others acknowledged to prove they were nice to minorities and the less fortunate.

"Dude," Brian said as he slid into the seat across from Theo.

"You are never going to guess what just happened to me." Theo told him about Jackie Leonard.

"This must be some alternate universe," Brian said. "Up is down, down is up. Jackie invites a card-carrying nerd to Disneyland?" He shook his head. "Maybe they intend to abandon you there. Maroon you in the *Pirates of the Caribbean* ride. Superglue your butt to the seat at Space Mountain. There has to be a catch."

"I think it's because—wait for it—I'm on the basketball team."

Brian shook his head. "Is this going to be one of those teen stories where the nerd suddenly becomes popular and then leaves all his nerdy friends behind?"

"Man, I hope so."

Brian laughed. "Jerk."

"Moron."

"Loser."

"Loser Plus."

They laughed again. Then Theo noticed that Brian's tray wasn't the usual assortment of Fried Whatever and Fattening Goo. He had a paper bag from which he unpacked a banana, a granola bar, a carton of 2 percent milk, and a small box of raisins. He carefully laid them out on his tray. Then he picked up the banana, peeled it, and took a bite. Theo just stared, like an anthropologist who has discovered a strange, primitive tribe that eats skunks.

"Where'd you get that stuff?" he asked.

"Rain." He took another bite of banana, and then shook some raisins into his palm. "She caught me coming out of physical science, handed me the bag, and said, 'You don't always have to be such a pig, you know?'"

"What? She said that?"

Brian laughed. "Yeah, I know. Smooth talker. I almost threw the bag at her." He ripped open the granola bar, took a bite. "Yum, peanut butter."

Theo looked around the crowd to see if Rain was watching her handiwork, but he couldn't spot her anywhere. Why had she done this for Brian? Why were his eating habits suddenly her business? Brian's parents were always trying to get him to go on a diet. His mom had tried every diet in existence, and even took him along to some of her Weight Watchers meetings. But nothing had worked.

"I don't get it, dude. You've always made fun of the diets your parents put you on. Now all of a sudden some strange—and I mean *seriously* strange—girl hands you a bag of food and you're on a diet?"

Brian shrugged. "I guess so."

"Why now? Why her? Do you *like* her?"

Brian chewed thoughtfully. "Yeah, she's cool and all, but that's not the only reason. I just keep thinking, she put all this effort into it. I mean, she assembled this lunch and carried it to school, waited outside my classroom to give it to me. Just for me. Why'd she even bother?"

Theo watched his friend devour the raisins, tearing apart the box so he could unstick the last one from the cardboard. He doubted this was the beginning of a new, improved Slim Brian. By tomorrow he'd be back to gorging on fries and shakes. But the thing that really bothered Theo was this: Why hadn't *he* been the one to hand him that bag? Why hadn't *he* made more of an effort to help his friend all these years?

"Maybe you liked having a fat sidekick," Brian said.

"What?" Theo said, startled.

He laughed. "You're not exactly a closed book, dude. You've been watching me eat with the sad eyes usually found on basset hounds and toddlers with full diapers. You were wondering why you never encouraged me to go on a diet. Or to stick with one my parents were cramming down my throat instead of food."

"Are you saying I wanted you to stay fat?"

"We fatties don't like that term. We prefer 'horizontally challenged.' 'Abdominally impaired.' Or 'chublicious.'" He punched Theo in the arm lightly. "Ease up, man. I'm only kidding. I was the fat Jewish kid and you were the skinny black kid. A politically correct version of Laurel and Hardy. Neither of us wanted the formula to change. If I thought sitting on your head would have kept you from growing six inches, I'd still be perched there right now."

But Theo had grown. And other things were changing,

too. Things at home. Things at school. Things with Brian. The more Theo grew up, the more his world grew out of his control.

Speaking of things being out of control, he told Brian about his encounter with Motorpsycho and his shadowy pal.

Brian got angry. "Seriously, dude, does your flipping phone not work? And don't give me another blow-off about your dad's online dating life."

"Yeah, about that." And he told Brian about Miranda Sanjume and his dad's mysterious late-night meeting.

Brian just stared at him. "And you didn't think *that* was worth a call? This from the guy who talked to me for twenty minutes when he discovered his first chest hair?"

"I'm sorry I didn't call. I'm just trying to figure things out."

"Forget about Marcus's love life for a moment. More important, a guy threatens you and your dad and you don't tell Marcus, let alone me? That's stupid."

"I wanted to talk to Rain first. Hear her explanation."

Brian grinned. "Oh, I get it now. You're afraid she's somehow mixed up in something bad and you might get her in trouble if you tell."

Actually, he hadn't thought of that, but once Brian had said it aloud, he realized it was probably true. Which confused him even more. He didn't owe her anything.

"It's okay, man. You like her. It was bound to happen sooner or later."

"I don't 'like' her. I don't dislike her. She's . . . weird."

"Yeah, but good weird. Like us."

They ate in silence for a few minutes. Then they switched the subject from Rain to the Brain Train. They had a practice session after lunch and Theo really needed it to go well. He needed to focus, not think about Rain, or basketball, or his dad's dating, or Motorpsycho's threats. Just science.

"Want me to quiz you?" Brian offered.

"Yeah, thanks," Theo said. "Want my apple?"

"Sure," Brian said, and quickly snatched it from Theo's hand. "I'm starving." He bit into it with a ravenous smile.

WHEN Theo and Brian arrived at Mr. J's classroom for Brain Train practice, they were surprised to see Rain sitting in the second row next to Daryl and Tunes. (More than surprised. Surprised would be finding a human ear in your cereal bowl. This was much worse.)

Rain sat primly with her hands on top of the desk like she was Little Miss Sunshine instead of Wanted-by-Motorpsycho Crazy Girl. She wore a yellow T-shirt with small black letters spelling out NO LOGO.

"What are you doing here?" Theo blurted.

"It's a free country," she said with a smile.

Theo scowled. Some things shouldn't be free. The Brain Train was his Fortress of Solitude, his escape from the rest of the world. The kids in this room might all be rats-gnawing-on-their-brains strange, but they were Theo's kind of strange. The predictable kind that he understood. They were all about facts, things that could be measured, recorded, and recited. Rain was about . . . He couldn't think of the right word. Maybe there was no word for what she was. Which is why she made him so crazy.

"Seriously," he said, trying to stay calm, "why are you here?"

Mr. J appeared from his private office and answered for Rain. "Cerebral warriors, this is Rain Kadinski, a transfer student from Westlake. She's thinking of joining the Brain Train—"

Brooke's hand shot up like a rocket. "Mr. J!"

"—as a *junior alternate*," Mr. J finished.

Brooke's hand went down.

Mr. J continued: "She just wants to see what the team is like first, so I invited her to watch you guys in action. Informative for her and good practice for you to have an audience. Win-win."

Rain smiled brightly, like she was running for class president. "Thank you, Mr. J. You've been super helpful."

Super helpful? Who was she pretending to be now, Mary Poppins?

"I've got to grab the new supplements to your study manuals," Mr. J said. "So keep it down till I get back." He went to his private office, where he kept his personal computer and all the dangerous chemicals the students weren't allowed to handle without his supervision. (Rumor had it that he also had a Lucite paperweight in there that encased the severed finger of one of the students he'd blown to bits.)

Once Mr. J had disappeared through the door, Theo slid into the desk beside Rain's and demanded, "What are you doing here? You still stalking me?"

"It's not always about you, Theo," she said. "I'm interested in joining the team, that's all. Make new friends, expand my mind."

Theo leaned closer and whispered, "You said you'd tell me about Motorpsycho today. What does he want from you?"

"Not now," she whispered back. She gestured at all the people around them. "It's not the right time."

"When *will* it be the right time? When he's dragging our limp bodies down a gravel road behind his motorcycle?"

Suddenly Daryl slapped Theo on the back. "'Pull yourself together, Teddy! Pull yourself together.'"

"What?" Theo said, annoyed.

Rain laughed and said, "'It's the water. It's a lot of water.' *Shutter Island*, right? With Leo DiCaprio."

Daryl and Tunes stared at Rain as if she'd just floated into the room on a cloud.

"You can quote Lord Leo?" Tunes asked, his voice soft with awe.

She nodded. "'I know how to find secrets from your mind. I know all the tricks.' From *Inception*."

"'What's the most resilient parasite?'" Daryl quoted, challenging her.

"'An idea,'" Rain responded.

Daryl and Tunes looked at her, at each other, then at her again. If Rain had wanted to start a cult in which followers wore bologna pants and worshipped snot, she had two willing, dues-paying members right in front of her.

"What's with the shirt?" Brian asked. "Yesterday it said 'less.'"

"It's a good message, isn't it?" she said. "What most people want in life is 'more.'" She used finger quotes. "More TVs, more cars, more money. More stuff. Instead of thinking about what they *want*, they should think about what they *need*. Which is less."

"Oh, brother," Brooke scoffed. "What a load of crap."

"I think it's cool," Daryl said.

"Yeah, cool," Tunes concurred.

Of course, Rain could have said the world was flat as a pizza and revolved around a sun made of a tuna salad and fingernail clippings and they would have agreed. The boys were a little hypnotized by her.

Daryl pointed at Rain. "What's that one mean? 'No logo.'"

"It's a protest against kids being brainwashed into consumerism. I got it from a book by Naomi Klein."

Daryl and Tunes looked blank.

Rain explained, "Look, why should you pay to wear clothes that show the company's logo? You're paying them to advertise their product. But the companies have made the labels a status thing, so, like a bunch of mindless robots, we show off their labels. I think all labels should be removed from the outside of clothing."

Tunes looked thoughtful. "I think I saw something about that book on Radiohead's website."

"That's right," Rain said. "They were going to call their *Kid A* album *No Logo* after the book."

"Wow," Daryl said. "Radiohead."

"And rapper MC Lars has a song called 'No Logo' after the book. People are getting the word." Rain smiled.

"The word," Brooke muttered with a sarcastic snort. The official snort judges would have given that one a 9.9.

"Where do you get them?" Tunes asked. "Urban Outfitters?"

"I make them. I think of them as one-word poems, but this time I used two words. Special case. I can make one for you if you want."

"Cool," Tunes said.

"You know," Daryl said proudly, "I've been working on a project myself."

Brian, Tunes, and Theo groaned in harmony.

"Shut up!" Daryl said to them. Then back to Rain, "It's a Taser cookbook. I'm trying to figure out recipes of foods you can cook using a Taser. Like hot dogs and stuff."

"Why not use a microwave?"

Daryl frowned at her as if she'd just sneezed in his face. "Obviously, 'cuz Tasing food is more fun."

"I can see that," Rain said.

Daryl grinned sheepishly, as if she'd just kissed him on the cheek.

Unable to contain his impatience any longer, Theo jerked his head for Rain to follow him to the back of the room. He felt everyone watching them as they turned their backs and whispered.

"What's going on with that motorcycle guy? Tell me *right now.*"

Rain sighed and looked down. "Okay, okay. His name is Milos. Like I said before, he's my cousin from Lithuania. The Gypsy side of my family. He and the rest of his Gypsy family are here running a kidnapping ring. They want me to identify children who would bring a big ransom." She nodded toward Brooke. "Like her. He wants my list of names."

Theo's jaw must have thudded against his chest. "What? Gypsies kidnapping kids? Really?"

Rain laughed. "No, not really, you moron. That's the plot of some TV movie I saw once. Man, you are way too easy." She returned to her seat just as Mr. J returned.

"Come and get 'em, hot off the griddle," Mr. J said, passing out the study-guide supplements.

Brooke immediately began thumbing through her copy. Tunes and Daryl rolled theirs up and started sword-fighting with them.

"Okay, okay," Mr. J said, "let's put them away and get down to the business of putting old heads on young shoulders."

Brian raised his hand. "'Old heads on young shoulders.' It's what Jean Brodie says about teaching in the novel *The Prime of Miss Jean Brodie* by Scottish writer Muriel Spark, adapted into a 1969 film starring Maggie Smith, who played Professor McGonagall in the Harry Potter movies." He grinned and looked around the room for acknowledgment of his brilliance.

All he got was Tunes pretend-coughing, "Show-off."

Mr. J said, "And what does it mean to put old heads on young shoulders?"

"It means to put knowledge and wisdom into young kids' brains."

"Very good, Brian," Mr. J said, clapping his hands. "Now, *that* is how you answer a question. As you all know, the judges award one to ten points for each answer based on accuracy, thoroughness, and clarity. That, my friends, is a ten-point answer."

Brian beamed and snapped his fingers at Tunes. "Booyah, bro."

"Brooke," Mr. J said, "what does *sic semper tyrannis* mean to you?"

Brooke rolled her eyes to show that the question was beneath her. "It's Latin. Means 'thus ever to tyrants.' First used by Brutus when he assassinated Julius Caesar. Later spoken by John Wilkes Booth after assassinating President Lincoln on April fourteenth, 1865." She smirked in triumph and waited for the praise to be heaped upon her like fairy dust.

Mr. J smiled. "Very impressive, Brooke. Adding the date of the assassination was a good touch. Just what the judges are looking for. In fact, you—"

"Excuse me, Mr. J," Rain said, raising her hand.

Uh-oh, Theo thought. Cancel the fairy dust, pass out the helmets. Bombs were about to fall.

"Yes, Rain?" Mr. J said.

"I don't know if this is important, because I've never been to one of these Aca-lympic competitions, but how thorough does an answer have to be?"

"What do you mean?" Mr. J asked.

"Well, for example, regarding Brooke's answer . . ."

Brooke's head swiveled toward Rain, her eyes firing laser beams.

"Would it be relevant to say that *sic semper tyrannis* is also the state motto of Virginia? And that Timothy McVeigh, the guy convicted of setting off that bomb in Oklahoma, was wearing a T-shirt with a picture of Lincoln and *sic semper tyrannis* on it the day he was arrested?"

Mr. J smiled like a guy who's just found a hundred-dollar bill on the street. "Well, well, well, we might just have a serious contender here."

Theo just stared at Rain. Who was this girl who knew so much and who had so many mysteries? At that moment, there was something so compelling about her that he couldn't take his eyes off of her. It wasn't just her looks (okay, twist his arm and he'd admit that she was cute), it wasn't just her knowledge (which he was starting to think might be even greater than his own), it was the fearless-ness with which she spoke. Like she was daring anyone to disagree.

"I knew all that!" Brooke screeched, her face as red as a baboon's behind. "I just didn't think it was important."

Mr. J ignored Brooke. "What subject is your specialty, Rain?"

Rain shrugged. "I don't know yet. Lots of stuff interests me."

Yeah, like criminals on motorcycles, Theo thought.

"Ah, a Renaissance woman. Delightful."

Brooke, unable to endure Rain being praised, burst out with, "Mr. J, I think my answer is much better than hers. The judges would have accepted it and awarded us ten points. In fact, they would have preferred its relevancy to the ramblings of our underdressed and overpraised guest."

Mr. J (to Rain): "What's your response?"

Rain: "Sure, whatever. I'm just here to observe. 'I wear the mask. It does not wear me.'"

Brooke: "What does that even mean?"

Daryl and Tunes giggled and high-fived.

Daryl: "It means she's awesome, Brooke. She just quoted Sir Leo as Philippe in *The Man in the Iron Mask*."

Brooke (slightly hysterical): "This is ridiculous! I'm sitting here with a bunch of morons that want to talk about Leo DiCrappy-o and Taser cookbooks and homemade T-shirts that say absolutely nothing while an aging hippie teacher does nothing to stop it."

Someone hit the pause button and the world froze.

Oh no, she di-n't! Theo thought.

Everyone turned to Mr. J to see what his reaction would be. Detention? Disbanding the Brain Train? Encase everyone in Lucite?

Instead, Mr. J just chuckled. "Now that was a good speech, Brooke. Very entertaining. Insulting, but still witty. I'd give that one a nine-point-eight."

Everyone—including Brooke—sighed with relief that the giant meteor had passed without smashing into Earth and destroying their lives.

Suddenly Daryl raised his hand. Theo groaned inwardly. Sometimes when Daryl got a thought in his head he couldn't relax until he'd expressed it.

"Say, Mr. J," Daryl asked, "*are* you a hippie?"

And the meteor turned around and headed straight for Earth again.

"Yes, Daryl, I am a hippie. I hug trees, even the ones that ask me not to. I resist clubbing baby seals whenever I see one, even the ones that deserve clubbing. I sleep in pajamas made entirely of flowers and good wishes."

Everyone laughed. Except Brooke.

"I also marched with Martin Luther King Jr. in support of civil rights, and I protested against the Vietnam War. Man, those were some crazy times."

Brooke: "You're too young to have done that."

Mr. J: "You're right, I am. I guess that wasn't me. Which makes me wonder why you think I'm a hippie?"

Daryl shrugged. "Your hair. The posters. The way you

act, all . . . hippielike." He shrugged. "Mostly the hair."

Mr. J: "If I didn't have 'the hair,' would you still have asked if I was a hippie?"

Daryl didn't say anything. Theo could see he sensed a trap.

Mr. J went to his desk, rummaged inside the drawer, and came up with a huge pair of scissors. Then he grabbed his ponytail and started cutting. The students—even Brooke and Rain—stared in disbelief. It took almost a minute for him to saw through the thick hair. When he was done, he used the rubber band that had held the ponytail together to bind the cut hair into one clump. He tossed it onto Daryl's desk.

Mr. J: "There you go. Now I'm not a hippie. Right?"

No one said anything. They'd never seen a teacher do anything so radical in a class. Once, in drama, Mr. Bandeer had burped the alphabet, but that was it.

Theo: "Mr. J, are you all right? You aren't having a stroke or something, are you?"

Mr. J laughed. "I'm fine, everybody. I just cut off some hair. You act like I stabbed my dog."

Tunes raised his hand. "Mr. J, I have the feeling this was supposed to be some kind of lesson. Teachers never do anything unless there's some Big Message attached. But I don't get it. What's the lesson?"

Theo didn't get it either, but he didn't want to admit it in front of Rain.

Mr. J: "No lesson. I've had long hair since high school, and I wondered what I'd look like without it. I took a leap of faith."

Tunes: "A what of who?"

"A leap of faith. That's when you do something risky because it's more important to see the outcome than to worry about looking foolish." He turned to Daryl. "Daryl, who invented the first mechanical calculator?"

Daryl: "Pascal."

Mr. J stared at him.

Daryl: "French mathematician and philosopher Blaise Pascal invented the mechanical calculator in 1642. It could add, subtract, and multiply." He looked at Rain as if expected her to disagree. She didn't.

And so it went for the next half hour, with most of the questions going to Daryl and Tunes. They knew the answers, though Mr. J had to keep prompting Daryl to expand on his responses. Occasionally, he would whip a question at Brooke, and she would reply calmly and coolly with a thorough answer.

Theo was relieved that Mr. J was ignoring him. Despite his every intention to study more, he was so far behind that he wasn't sure he could do well today. Maybe Mr. J was trying to protect him from Brooke's attacks. Maybe Mr. J really was his friend after all.

Theo looked at the wall clock. Three minutes until algebra. Three minutes until safety.

Then, like a sudden crack of thunder on a sunny summer day, Mr. J's voice split the air. "Well now, Theo, let's see whether you still have a place on this team."

Theo's stomach lurched as if it had been Tased for Daryl's cookbook.

MR. J: "First question: Why is bird poop white?"

Everyone looked at Theo expectantly.

Theo: "Because birds don't pee."

Tunes: "Mr. J, should he say 'urinate' instead of 'pee'? What will the judges want?"

Mr. J: "'Pee' is fine. Continue, Theo."

Tunes and Daryl snickered.

Mr. J waited, his eyes fixed on Theo. No one else moved or breathed. The only sound was the squeaking of Brooke's bright red lips sliding across her shiny teeth as she formed a nasty grin—though Theo may have imagined that.

Theo (after a deep breath): "Birds' kidneys extract nitrogenous wastes from the bloodstream like ours do, but they don't dissolve it in urine like we do. It comes out of the cloaca, which they use to both poop and pee, as a white paste."

Daryl and Tunes snickered again at the poop and pee talk.

Mr. J: "Theo, what is the most expensive substance in the world?"

For a moment, Theo's mind went blank; all he could think of was *popcorn at the movies*. Then he remembered (he hoped).

"Californium. A radioactive substance used in starting nuclear reactors. It costs about twenty-seven million dollars a gram. A gram is about the same weight as a paper clip."

Mr. J nodded. "Nicely done. The paper-clip reference was a nice touch."

Theo nodded back, his mouth too dry to respond. Fortunately, he'd just read about bird poop and Californium last night. Thank goodness Mr. J had not gone deeper into the study material, because Theo was about fifty pages behind.

Mr. J: "Tunes, Mozart composed his first complete symphony at what age?"

Tunes (formally, as if talking to the police): "Mozart composed Symphony No. 1 in E Flat when he was eight."

Mr. J: "At what age did he write his first minuet?"

Tunes: "Mozart wrote his first minuet at six. He died when he was thirty-five, but he was so poor that he was buried in a mass grave. No one knows for sure where he was buried."

Mr. J: "While all that is true, Tunes, his death wasn't part of the question. Don't pad your answers with irrelevant details. The judges will deduct points. Theo, what information should he have included?"

Theo: "What a minuet is."

Mr. J: "Exactly."

Tunes (still robotically): "A minuet is a social dance for two people, usually in three-quarter time. It originated with the French."

Theo looked at the clock. Two minutes left. He'd made it. He'd bluffed his way through practice, securing his place for another day. Tonight he could catch up on the study guides.

Everyone had started to gather up their books and backpacks when Mr. J held up his hand and said, "Theo, tell me everything you know about Scarabaeoidea. You have one minute."

Theo felt as if someone had just reached into his stomach to yank out his intestines.

Theo: [Silence]

Mr. J: "Do you need me to repeat the question?

Theo shook his head, but didn't answer.

Daryl, Tunes, Brooke, Rain: [Deafening silence]

Theo rummaged through his brain like a thief searching a house for valuables. He came up empty. The question was from the material he had not yet read.

Brian: "Mr. J, why are all your questions to Theo about poop and pee? Not that I'm complaining, because it's funny as heck—I'm just curious."

Thank you, Brian, Theo thought, knowing Brian was trying to stall Mr. J and give Theo time to think.

Mr. J: "Which logical fallacy did Brian just express?"

Brooke: "Hasty generalization. He drew a conclusion

from a small sample—in this case, just two out of the dozens of questions asked today."

Mr. J: "Correct. Now, Theo, has Brian's diversion given you enough time to come up with an answer?"

Theo: "No. I don't know the answer."

Mr. J: "Anyone else? I realize that you all study only your own subjects, but this is a good one for general knowledge."

No one raised a hand. When the kids in this group didn't know an answer, they looked down like a dog in shame for chewing the TV remote. Everyone looked down. Except Rain.

Mr. J: "The dung beetle feeds mostly on poop. The Scarabaeoidea is the superfamily, composed of five thousand species. Some dung beetles roll big balls of dung wherever they go, which they use for food and breeding...."

Theo's heart pounded so loudly in his ears that he barely heard the rest of what Mr. J said. Something about how these poop-pushers were called scarabs in ancient Egypt, and they were considered sacred, which he knew from the *Mummy* movies. The Egyptians thought their rolling balls of dung resembled the god Khepri, who rolled the sun across the sky every day. Crazy stuff like that.

When Mr. J was done, he turned to Theo again and asked, "What causes champagne to fizz when it's poured into a glass?"

Theo looked at the clock. One minute. Could he stall for one minute? Not with the way Mr. J was staring at him.

Theo: "Carbon dioxide?"

Mr. J: "No. The fizz occurs when it comes in contact with dust or dirt particles in the glass. If the glass were completely free of dust molecules, the champagne would be still."

Daryl: "Are you allowed to ask us questions about alcohol?"

Mr. J: "Theo, paper or plastic?"

Theo: "Huh?"

Mr. J: "Which is better for the environment?"

Theo (guessing): "Paper?"

Mr. J: "Nope. Manufacturing paper bags requires more energy than manufacturing plastic bags. Recycling paper also requires more energy than recycling plastic."

Theo (struggling to save face): "But paper is more biodegradable."

Mr. J: "Wrong again. Since landfills are mostly airtight beneath the surface, neither plastic nor paper biodegrades."

The silence was weird. It was as if they'd just been told Taylor Swift had been arrested for punching a baby.

Brooke raised her hand. "Mr. J, I think it's clear that Theo is not taking the Brain Train seriously and it's time to replace him with Constance Rodriguez. She's been studying the science manual and is not only caught up but has read far ahead."

Theo held his breath, hoping Mr. J would dismiss Brooke's attempts at assassination. The bell to change classes sounded before the teacher could reply.

Saved by the bell, Theo thought, grabbing his backpack.

"Hold on, everybody," Mr. J said.

Everyone froze.

Theo's legs went numb and he sat back down.

Mr. J: "Theo, I've been warning you that this could happen."

Theo: "I've fallen a little behind because of basketball. I can catch up."

Mr. J: "How? Have you quit basketball?"

Theo: "No. I'll just try harder."

Brooke: "Too late. We have to face Lansing in two weeks, and Constance is ready now."

Mr. J picked up his severed ponytail and smacked it a few times against the palm of his hand.

Suddenly Rain said, "Why not have a showdown, Mr. J? Constance versus Theo. The winner is on the first team."

Theo spun to glare at Rain, but she ignored him, waiting for Mr. J's answer.

Brooke didn't know what to say to that.

In the hall, students were passing noisily to their next class. Mr. J didn't have a class this period, but the others would all be late if they didn't leave now.

"Done!" Mr. J said. "Friday morning, right here, we will have a showdown between Theo and Constance. May the most prepared win."

Friday? Theo already had a Friday deadline from Motorpsycho.

Outside the classroom, he pulled Rain aside. Brian,

Daryl, and Tunes formed a semicircle around her. From his height, Theo could see Brooke grabbing Constance out of the stream of students. Undoubtedly, she would be quizzing Constance every possible minute until Friday.

"Why'd you do that?" Theo asked Rain.

"I saved you," Rain said. "He was about to kick you to the curb, dude."

"True dat," Daryl agreed.

Theo said, "No one says 'true dat' anymore."

Daryl frowned. "Really? I like 'true dat.' I'll miss it. Maybe it can be a retro thing."

"I'm going to be late," Rain said, starting for class. The boys followed.

Daryl smiled. "I'm going to bring 'true dat' back. I'll make it a campaign. Posters. A website."

"Why a showdown?" Theo asked. Meaning: he didn't want to be humiliated in public.

Rain stopped and faced him. "Look, Brooke is going to be on your case every day until Mr. J gets rid of you."

"She's evil," Brian said.

"But is she wrong?" Rain said. This was the second time she had asked that question. Whose side was she on?

The boys didn't respond. Theo realized why. Brooke wasn't wrong.

Rain walked away. Over her shoulder she said, "You have to step up, Theo, if you want Brooke to lay off. Mean-time, we have to stop her, in public. 'When you kill a king, you don't stab him in the dark. You kill him where the entire court can watch him die.'"

Tunes chuckled gleefully. "Dude, she just quoted Saint Leo in *Gangs of New York*! How awesome is that?"

Daryl shouted after Rain, "You realize in four years you're going to have to go to prom with all of us."

"I know just the T-shirt I'll wear," Rain said as she walked away.

Tunes grinned. "She didn't say no."

"True dat," Daryl said.

"MR. Hudson?" Weston Zheng said without raising his hand. Weston never raised his hand. When he had something to say, he just said it. Didn't matter who else was talking, even Mr. Hudson (who had been, in fact, discussing S. E. Hinton's novel *The Outsiders*, something about conflict in Ponyboy and Sodapop's relationship).

"Yes, Weston." Mr. Hudson lowered the book. The muscles at the back of his jaw flexed in anticipation. Weston never answered questions, even those directly asked by teachers, so they no longer bothered to ask him any. Weston only spoke when he wanted something.

Weston got away with it because his mom was the president of the PTA and his dad's face was on about a thousand real estate signs in the area. This was only middle school, but a lot of the adults already knew which students were going to be the hotshots of the future. Mr. Hudson was still in his twenties, so he'd probably be around to teach Weston's kids someday. He didn't want to risk any grief now or later. These were, after all, dangerous times of teacher layoffs.

"Uh, basketball practice is early today, so can me and Theo leave?"

"Now?" Mr. Hudson said, making a show of checking his watch. Class had only begun ten minutes ago.

"We have a big game coming up Friday."

"But it's only Tuesday," Mr. Hudson pointed out.

"Coach wants us to get a few extra practices in. Right, Theo?"

Theo heard a sound come out of his own mouth. It might have been a groan. Or a squeak like a rabbit might make when a drooling timber wolf has him cornered.

This wasn't the first time that Weston had asked to leave early. Usually, he pulled from a grab bag of reasons: dental appointment, doctor's appointment, therapist's appointment, family vacation in Hawaii. This was the first time he'd used basketball practice as his excuse. And it was the first time he had included Theo.

Theo finally found his voice. "I don't think Coach—"

Then Theo saw the panic in Mr. Hudson's eyes. He had been about to contradict Weston and say that he didn't know anything about an early practice. But that wasn't what Mr. Hudson wanted to hear. He wanted to put on a show of being annoyed, but he didn't want to actually catch Weston in a lie and deal with the political fallout. If Theo told the truth, Mr. Hudson would have no choice but to investigate, which would lead to a parent–teacher conference, which would put Mr. Hudson, his wife, and his three-month-old daughter in the sights of a powerful family.

Theo cleared his throat and started again. "I don't think Coach would want us to be late."

Mr. Hudson's body seemed to sag in relief. His voice was stern, but also a little shaky, when he said, "Okay, go on. But don't make it a habit."

"Thanks, Mr. Hudson," Weston said, already on his way out the door.

Theo quickly gathered his books, notebooks, and pencils and hurried after Weston. Weston hadn't bothered to take out any materials in class, so he was able to make a clean getaway.

Once outside, Theo felt a hand grab his arm and yank him to the wall. "Dude, you almost ruined everything," Weston growled.

"Sorry."

"No worries, man. It's all good." He slapped Theo on the shoulder as if they were old friends instead of guys who'd never spoken more than ten words to each other. The ten words that had been spoken had all come from Weston on the court, and they included such classics as "Stop dogging it!" and "You suck, dude!" and the ever-popular "Play D, dawg!"

They headed silently toward the gym. In movies, schools were usually big boxes with hallways jammed with kids changing classes. In Orange County, most schools looked like spiders, with the principal's office and front desk where the spider's body would be, and all the classrooms radiating outward like legs. Each classroom had two doors, one that opened to the hallway, and another that opened to the outside. Since it was almost always sunny, students usually used the door to the outside.

Weston and Theo walked past classroom after classroom jammed with imprisoned students. The kids inside watched them with obvious envy. Theo had to admit that seeing them trapped at their desks while he strolled freely across the grass gave him a feeling of power and privilege. He suddenly realized he liked power and privilege.

"So, I heard you were in some kinda fight at the park," Weston said.

"Not really. I accidentally bumped a kid during a basketball game, and he took a swing at me."

Weston nodded, as if giving each word considerable thought. "I've never been in a fight, 'cept with my brother. My dad says he was in lots of fights when he was a kid."

"Mine, too."

"What was it like? Were you scared?"

"Yeah. But also relieved." Until Theo had said those words, he hadn't realized it himself.

"Relieved? What do you mean?"

"I don't know. I guess you grow up hearing about your dad getting into fights, so you figure it's inevitable. One day you're going to have to fight. You build it up in your mind, worry about whether you'll lose an eye, or accidentally kill somebody. I don't know. It's just that now I did it and it's over, I don't have to worry about it anymore."

Weston nodded again. "Hey, maybe we should get in a

fight right now. Then I won't have to worry about it."

Theo gulped. "What?"

Weston punched him lightly in the arm. "Just kidding, dude. I don't want to mess up this beautiful face."

Theo forced a laugh and they continued on to the gym. For the rest of the walk, Weston told dead-baby jokes.

Weston led Theo around the back of the building, which was out of sight of the classrooms. Some of their teammates—Chris, Roger, and Sinjin—were already there. If this had been a teen movie, they'd be smoking or drinking beer. Instead, they were leaning against the wall and talking basketball.

Chris was describing some play from a pro game the night before. Theo didn't recognize any names of the players or the teams. So he listened to the other boys talk stats and shots and team trades without contributing anything but an occasional enthusiastic nod. Yet, even though they seemed to be speaking a foreign language, he wasn't bored. It was exciting to leave his nerdy self behind for a change. He made a mental note to start following the sport so that next time he could join the conversation.

If there *was* a next time, he corrected himself. Unless he could bring it on the court at practice, he doubted he'd ever hang with this group again.

COACH: "Theo, hustle, hustle, hustle! You're running like you've got a load in your pants."

Coach: "No, no, no, Theo, you can't move your pivot foot."

Coach: "Theo, pull the ball tighter to your chest. That's why they keep stealing it from you. You hold it out like you're offering free samples of yogurt at the mall."

Theo did his best to correct his mistakes. But he just kept making new ones. In one play, Weston was dribbling toward the basket. Theo was guarding him, sliding, sliding, sliding, arms waving. Suddenly he slid into a brick wall and went down, his arms and legs folding up like a Swiss Army knife. He'd run into Roger McDonald's two hundred pounds. Weston scored.

"Oops." Roger smirked. He high-fived Sinjin.

Everyone scored. Everyone who Theo guarded.

Coach ended practice as he always did, with rounds of Sudden Death. Each boy was paired with another boy. One boy played defense, the other offense. The boy with the ball had one minute to score as many points as possible.

Then they switched. The loser sat, the winner advanced, until there was only one. Like in *Highlander*.

Theo was paired against Roger, the slowest guy on the team, but also the heaviest. Theo decided to use his height advantage. He immediately drove to the hoop, hoping to get close enough to lob it in over Roger's large, square head. But Roger stopped him ten feet from the hoop and kept his arm bar buried so deep in Theo's spine that Theo thought it might be fused to his back. Theo tried to spin around him, but Roger just slid over and stood his ground. Roger might have been slow as a glacier, but he was also as hard to get around. In the end, Theo just took a couple desperate ten-foot shots, missing both.

Roger, on the other hand, hit two shots from the free throw line. Theo was the first to be eliminated. And the only one to score no points.

At the end of practice, an exasperated Coach called everyone over to the bleachers.

"Boys, I think you'll all agree that we need to step it up if we're going to beat Lemon Hill Friday. They're very, very good. They can shoot, sure, but so can you. They're fast, but I think you guys, as a team, are faster. The main advantage they have right now is size. They are a little bigger than you."

Theo waited for someone on the team to point to him and say, "We have our own big man." But no one did.

Chris Richards said, "What's our strategy, Coach? How are we going to counter their size advantage?"

Coach stroked his goatee. "We stick to the plan. As a team, they're bigger than us, but Theo is still taller than any one of their players. That gives us a slight advantage on the inside. So, we'll just have to outplay them. They're big, so they're bound to be a little overconfident. That could turn out to be their weakness. We pass the ball, try to split the defense, and be patient when shooting. We wait for the open shot. Hopefully, Theo will help give us those open shots."

The boys all nodded at the wisdom of that strategy, so Theo nodded, too.

"All right, everybody," Coach said, "see you tomorrow."

Everyone headed to the locker room.

"Theo." Coach waved for Theo to stay behind.

"Yeah, Coach?" Theo said brightly, trying to show as much enthusiasm as possible. Maybe if he pretended nothing was wrong, Coach wouldn't say anything about his abysmal performance during practice. He grabbed his towel and wiped his sweaty forehead.

Coach patted the wooden bleacher beside him. "Sit."

Theo sat. Was this the farewell speech as he got kicked off the team? During Sudden Death, he might have welcomed it. But right now, with the reality staring him in the face, he realized he wanted to be on this team more than anything. More than he wanted to be on Brain Train.

"You know what I like most about basketball, Theo?" Coach started.

Theo thought, If you're going to kick me off, do it

quickly, like yanking a Band-Aid. But he said, "No, Coach."

"Most players might say something like 'the thrill of competition,' or 'scoring that crucial point to win the game,' or 'playing in front of all those people.'"

"There were like thirty people at our last game, Coach."

Coach tugged on his goatee, a sure sign of annoyance.

Theo said, "Sorry. Go on."

"The thing that I most like about basketball is that no matter who you are, how much money your parents have, how good-looking you are, or how many statistics you've memorized about pro players, you are always judged by one thing and one thing only: how well you play the game. There is no past, no future. It doesn't matter how well you played yesterday or last week. It's how well you play today. Right now. On this court. In this particular game."

He paused, so Theo nodded.

"You see my point, Theo?"

"I think so. Basketball is like a democracy in which people are judged solely on merit."

Coach smiled broadly. "Right. That's right. Well said."

"I just don't see why you're telling me."

"Because, Theo, right now, right here on this court, you suck at basketball."

Theo surprised himself by laughing. "What was your first clue?"

Coach sighed, trying to find the right words. "The point is, you don't have to suck. You have potential, even if they"—he nodded toward the rest of the team already in the locker room—"or even you, don't see it right now. You're smart, analytical—"

"And tall."

"Yeah, you're tall, and that's a definite advantage. Don't let anyone tell you different. Sure, there are some excellent pros out there who are short by basketball standards, but they are the rarity. You're taller than everyone else here, but not taller than all the players your age. Every year it seems like the players are getting bigger. You saw the video of Mamadou N'Diaye. The dude is like Goliath."

"I'm sure glad we don't have to play against him," Theo said.

Coach stroked his goatee again as if it was a magic lamp and he wanted to wish that Theo were a better player. Then he suddenly changed the subject. "Look, Theo, I heard about your fight at the park."

Theo blinked, a little surprised that word of the incident had reached the coach's ears. "Not really a fight, Coach. One punch that barely grazed me. And I didn't hit him back. At best, an altercation."

"Listen, I appreciate that you're trying to sharpen your skills by playing pickup games. I did the same thing at the same park. Great place to learn and meet other kids."

Yeah, Theo thought, like Rain and Motorpsycho.

"Thing is, you can't get in fights and stay on the team. We have a zero-tolerance-for-violence policy. So be careful."

"But I didn't get into a fight. He punched *me*."

He shrugged. "School policy, Theo."

No point in arguing that, Theo thought. Once they pull out the old "school policy," the time for rational thought and intelligent debate is over. They make "policy" sound like some giant fire-breathing monster that lives in a nearby cave and is very sensitive to any insults from the villagers. If they say or do anything Policy doesn't like, he'll come crashing down on the town and burn everyone to a crisp.

"Theo," Coach said in a low voice, so low Theo had to lean in to hear him, "this isn't a race thing, is it?"

"What do you mean?" Theo asked, taken aback.

"You aren't trying to prove anything, are you? Being black doesn't mean you have to, you know, be a tough guy. Doesn't even mean you have to play basketball if you don't want to."

Coach stroked his goatee again. Each variation of stroking it expressed an entirely different emotion. This one was Teacher Concern.

"I'm not becoming Shaft, Coach, if that's what you mean," Theo said.

Coach smiled. "I dig the reference, Theo. I just . . . I just remember the pressure when I was one of only a handful of black kids at this school. Sometimes it was like everything I did was seen by others as a reflection of all black people. I hated that."

Theo nodded. He knew what the coach was talking about. Sometimes he felt like saying something mean to someone or skipping doing his homework. But he didn't because he had a feeling someone might think "Black people are mean" or "Black people are dumb." He'd talked with Brian about that and Brian had said he'd felt the same way, only about being Jewish. That everything he did or said could encourage some kids to hate Jews. Did Daryl feel that way about being Asian? Did Brooke feel that way about being a girl?

"Even if I did feel that way," Theo said, "there's nothing I can do about it, right? I mean, you feel the way you feel."

"You're right, you can't change the way you feel. But you can use it to motivate yourself to become a better person. The trick is that you still have to become your own person. Not just what others want or expect. Understand?"

Theo nodded. Theoretically, he did understand, though practically he still wasn't sure what his "own person" was yet. Adults liked to talk about this mythological Own Person, but they were always hazy on the details. Like most things, it seemed to come down to doing what they wanted you to do.

"All right," Coach said. "Good talk." His voice was back to normal volume and Theo understood that their private moment of sharing was now over.

Coach sent Theo to the locker room with a warning: "Just remember what I said, Theo. We'd certainly hate to lose you from the team."

"Are you going to kick me off the team if we don't win on Friday?" Theo asked.

Coach looked uncomfortable. Finally, he said, "Let's talk Friday after the game."

"So that's a yes," Theo persisted.

Coach didn't answer. He walked off toward his office.

Theo sat on the bleacher and looked around the gym. So far today he'd been threatened with expulsion from both teams he was on. He thought about his life without those teams and he felt a dark sadness tighten around his neck until it was hard to breathe.

After a long while, he got up and trudged to the locker room. The other players had already left, so he had the place to himself. He didn't mind; he didn't want to face them anyway.

After Theo changed clothes, he walked across campus to exit through the front entrance. When he stepped through the gate, he saw an unwelcome figure: Motorpsycho astride his big black motorcycle.

Motorpsycho pointed his leather-gloved finger at Theo, and then dragged the finger across his throat in a slicing motion. Then he revved his engine and took off with such a jolt of speed that the front of his motorcycle lifted in the air like Ghost Rider. The screech of tires echoed across the parking lot.

Very dramatic, Theo thought. Also, very effective.

Theo waited inside the school gate for twenty minutes before finally daring to leave. The walk home was about a mile and took just enough time for him to count all the reasons this was the worst Tuesday in the entire history of Tuesdays. And that included the stock market crash of 1929 (on a Tuesday) that started the Great Depression that devastated the entire country for a decade.

This Tuesday, Theo thought, is the beginning of my personal Great Depression. But Friday will be much, much worse.

Theo's Diary of Doom

1. Friday morning: Showdown with Constance to see if I get kicked off Brain Train.
2. Friday afternoon: Basketball game with Lemon Hill to see if I get kicked off the basketball team.
3. Friday after school: Avoid Motorpsycho, who wants to kick me out of living.
4. Friday night: Call Witness Protection and see if they have an opening.

The list reminded Theo of *The Three Musketeers*, which he'd read last year. In it, D'Artagnan is a young adventurer who goes to Paris to join the famous Musketeers. Only, he accidentally insults the men he idolizes, and he ends up with appointments to fight a duel with each of them—and they're all scheduled for the same time.

As Theo ran through all the ways his life could soon crash and burn, he felt his phone vibrate with a text message. He checked the screen.

CG (he really should change that): *What happened at bball today? You sucked worse than usual.*

Theo: *Thanks, stalker.*

CG: *They're gonna cut u, dude.*

Theo: *U were supposed to tell me about Motorpsycho today.*

CG: *No time. 2 busy saving your butt from getting cut from Brain Train. Seems like nobody wants u on their team.*

Theo: *U have time now. He was waiting for me after school. Gave me the death glare. Who is he and what does he want?????*

CG: *Not on phone. When I see u. Bye.*

She disconnected.

Brian texted a moment later. He wanted to know everything that was going on, so Theo told him, including the coach giving him until Friday to improve. And Motorpsycho's throat-cutting charade.

Theo: *3 showdowns on Friday. Should be called Black Friday.*

Brian: *Joke: What does a black guy call Black Friday?*

Theo: *I dunno.*

Brian: *Friday. Get it?*

Theo chuckled. Count on Brian to make him feel better. He promised to call him later and he turned the phone off.

Theo arrived home a minute later. He opened the front door with a sense of relief. Finally he had found his refuge from the cold, cruel world.

The relief lasted all of one second. That's when he saw Gavin standing in the living room, glowering at him.

"Hi, Gavin," Theo said, surprised. "What are you—"

"You lying, thieving jerk!" With that, Gavin hurled himself at Theo, tackled him to the ground, and wrapped his hands around his throat.

ADMITTEDLY, Theo wasn't much of a fighter. But as the air was being choked out of him, something caveman-ish kicked in, and he tried whatever he could to survive.

Like cry.

Scream.

Beg.

Since all of those are very hard to do without air, Theo switched tactics. However, those tactics were quite limited, given that he was flat on his back with the massive Gavin straddling him. Gavin's face was so scrunched with rage that it looked like a big clenched fist perched on top of his bulging neck. He yelled "Thief!" and "Liar!" and other nasty words with such fury that each one sprayed saliva in Theo's face.

Theo couldn't decide which was worse, the choking or the spitting. One was painful, the other gross. Then he realized that's the kind of debate you have when you're delirious from lack of oxygen.

Theo bucked up his hips to throw Gavin off, but the move barely budged his muscular cousin an inch. He grabbed Gavin's wrists and tried to pull them away, but Gavin was too strong. He reached up and wrapped his hands around Gavin's throat; Gavin's neck was so muscular it was like trying to squeeze a soccer ball.

Finally, he remembered a tip he had picked up from watching the spy show *Burn Notice*. On the show, the main character, ex-spy Michael Westen, gives all kinds of cool tips about how to break out of handcuffs, pick locks, make smoke bombs from peanut butter and mustard, and defeat much bigger attackers. In this case, all Theo had to do was peel back one pinkie finger and bend it until Gavin released both hands from his throat.

At first, it seemed to have no effect. Gavin kept his grip tight as a noose. So Theo bent the finger back even farther.

Gavin grunted and released that hand. He tried to jerk his pinkie free while keeping pressure on Theo's throat with his other hand. Theo continued to bend the finger.

Crack!

"Owww!" Gavin yelped and released Theo's throat. He jumped up and massaged his finger. "You could've broken it!"

Theo scrambled to his feet, coughing. "You could've killed me!" His voice was a little pinched from the choking.

"I wasn't going to kill you. Even though you deserve it." Gavin opened and closed his hand, wincing in pain.

"How do I deserve it? What did I do?"

"You ripped me off, man! You stole my music!"

"You gave me that CD," Theo said. "I didn't take it."

"Yeah, I gave it to you to listen to, not put on the Internet!"

Theo just stared. "What are you talking about?"

"Liar!" Gavin hollered, and charged at Theo again.

This time Theo was prepared. Just as Gavin threw his arm around Theo's head and pulled him into a headlock, Theo wrapped *his* arm around *Gavin's* head. They danced around in a double headlock, muttering curses and threats.

"What are you two doing?" boomed Theo's dad.

Both boys looked up to see Marcus standing in the doorway in his police uniform. They immediately released each other and stood up straight, almost at attention.

That's when they saw the person behind Marcus.

Theo recognized the woman instantly from the dating website.

Miranda Sanjume.

His dad's secret romance.

"JUST look!" Gavin said, searching YouTube for a video called "Wolfheart." "He's stolen my life!"

"'Wolfheart,'" Theo said. "That's the name of one of your songs on the CD."

"Brilliant deduction, Sherlock Homie," Gavin barked. "Especially since you're the one who stole it."

"Look, dude, for the last time: I didn't have anything to do with this."

"You're the only one who—"

Marcus clamped a strong hand on Gavin's shoulder. "Gavin, I think you know Theo well enough to know he's not a liar or a thief."

Theo tried not to melt into a puddle as he thought about how he had broken into his dad's private computer. The one they were now staring at. Wasn't that both lying and stealing?

"You're a cop, Uncle Marcus," Gavin said. "Just look at the evidence."

"Marcus," Miranda Sanjume said, pointing at the door, "I'll just let myself out. This doesn't seem like a good time. . . . Best of luck in solving the mystery."

Marcus nodded regretfully. "Sorry about the drama, Miranda. Life with teenagers, you know."

She smiled. "Call me later."

"Definitely," he said, with a grin that annoyed Theo. His dad was too old for goofy smiles around girls. "Have some dignity, Dad," he wanted to say.

"Nice meeting you boys," she said, waving as she left.

Gavin grumbled something that might have been "You, too," or "YouTube."

Theo said in his most polite voice, "Nice meeting you, Ms. Sanjume." He needed as many brownie points as he could get with his dad right now. After all, he was being accused of stealing.

Once the front door closed behind Miranda, Marcus turned his attention to the boys.

"Okay," he said, "let's watch the video and make sure it's the same song."

"I've watched it a hundred times," Gavin said.

Marcus gestured and Gavin clicked on play. The video was very simple—just four musicians playing the song in a poorly lit room. They looked like a typical rock band: shaggy long hair, jeans, a couple of flannel shirts, a couple of T-shirts, one leather jacket, and a jeans jacket. A lead guitar, rhythm guitar, bass, and drummer. Like the Beatles, Theo noted. The whole thing looked like it had been filmed on a phone by someone with a shaky hand.

There was no editing, no effects. Just the song. The lead singer had a deep, soulful voice, and when the other singer harmonized with him, goose bumps sprang up on Theo's neck.

When it was over, Marcus whistled appreciatively. "Man, they are good. I mean, *really* good." He looked at Theo for agreement. Theo gave Shrug Number 12: As a courtesy I won't disagree, but it ain't all that.

Marcus turned to Gavin. "You have to admit, they really do your song justice."

Gavin glared. "Doesn't matter. It's still *my* song!"

"Okay," Marcus said, all business. "Let's review the facts, just as with any crime scene. What do we know?"

Gavin scoffed. "We know a video was made by some band called Wild World singing 'Wolfheart.' We know I wrote 'Wolfheart.' We know that I didn't give the song to this band. We know they have no legal right to record it."

Marcus leaned over Gavin's shoulder and pointed at the screen. "We also know that since posting the video yesterday, they've had 56,432 views, with 20,398 Likes."

"Wow," Theo said with a whistle. "That's a lot of views for one day."

"I don't care how many views it gets!" Gavin said, pounding the desk so the mouse jumped. "You stole my song and sold it to them, punk!"

"I didn't steal your stupid song, moron!" Theo snapped back.

Marcus quickly jumped in. "Enough! Let's stick to the facts. Who is this band, uh . . ."—he looked at the computer screen—"Wild Wind?"

"Wild World," Gavin corrected. "I did some research. They're from down here, Orange County. They're pretty popular locally, and just starting to get some national attention. They have a deal with Big Dog Music to cut an album, and they'll be opening for Green Day this summer on tour."

"Green Day?" Theo said. "That's huge."

"I don't care how huge they are. They're still thieves, just like you, cuz."

Theo had had enough. He marched out of the room, grabbed his backpack from the living room, where he'd dropped it during their wrestling match, and brought it back to his dad's study. "Your stupid CD is right in here, where you stuck it. Which, by the way, I didn't ask for." He started digging through the bag.

"That being said," Marcus said, "your songs were pretty darn awesome, Gavin. I didn't know you had it in you, son."

Gavin started to say something, probably nasty. But then his expression softened and he just shrugged. "Thanks, Uncle Marcus."

"It's not here," Theo said in a panicky voice. "It's not here."

"What do you mean?" Gavin said.

"What do you think I mean, genius? 'It's not here'

means: It's. Not. Here. Your CD is not in my backpack." He upended it and dumped everything onto the floor. Textbooks, notebooks, pens, pencils, half a Snickers, and a few coins scattered across the beige carpet.

Gavin dropped to the floor and rummaged through Theo's school stuff. "Where is it, Theo? Who'd you give it to?"

"All right, all right," Marcus said, stepping between the two boys. "It's gone. Theo, when did you see it last?"

Theo told them about Tunes playing it in Mr. J's class.

"And you let him?" Gavin said, his eyes bulging as big as his biceps.

"He played it before I even knew he'd taken it. As soon as I knew, I told him to stop."

"So anyone in that class could have stolen it from your backpack afterward," Gavin said.

"Easy there, Michael Jackson," Theo said with a glare. "Don't start accusing my friends. Somebody out in the hall could have recorded it with their phone."

"Someone out in the hall?! How many people heard it?"

Theo explained about the kids who had gathered at the door to listen.

Gavin exploded. He jumped to his feet and kicked Theo's backpack across the room.

"Hey!" Theo said.

"Gavin," Marcus said sternly, "knock it off."

"But, Uncle Marcus, your son has ruined my life."

"Don't be such a drama queen," Theo said.

"Theo, be quiet," his dad scolded. To Gavin: "We'll get to the bottom of this. Look, even if you do decide to pursue legal action against Wild World, the longer it's on YouTube and getting hits, the more damages you can claim. Meantime, we need to get you on the next bus home so you don't miss school."

"But, Uncle Marcus—"

Marcus cut him off. "Do I look like I'm open to negotiation?"

Theo and Gavin studied Marcus's rock-hard cop face. He looked like he was ready to arrest both of them.

They drove Gavin to the bus terminal, where Marcus bought him a ticket back to Los Angeles. They watched him climb into the bus and settle into a window seat.

As Theo and his dad walked away, Theo looked over his shoulder and saw Gavin glaring at him through the glass. Gavin pointed at him and made a slicing motion across his throat. Just like Motorpsycho had done.

Seems to be a popular reaction to knowing me, thought Theo.

WEDNESDAY.

Back at school.

Two days before Friday. The End of the World.

How will it end for me? Theo wondered. Death by Motorpsycho? Death by Brain Train Showdown? Death by Basketball Game Loss?

Did the ancient Mayan calendar offer any clues?

What about the ancient Loser calendar?

Theo walked across the crowded parking lot as kids were dropped off at the curb. The long line of massive SUVs inching along the drop-off zone looked like a herd of hunched monsters belching out kids and crawling on.

Theo scanned the surroundings for Motorpsycho, but he didn't see him anywhere.

He sighed with relief. Finally, a break. A chance to catch his breath and think about—

Thwack.

A thick hand slapped him hard on the back, sending him stumbling forward a couple of awkward steps.

"Hey, little cousin," the familiar voice said. "Miss me?"

Theo spun around to see Gavin grinning.

"What are you doing here?" Theo demanded.

"Came to help you with the investigation of who stole my CD. That *is* what you were going to do today, right?"

Actually, Theo hadn't given it much thought. He had too many worries of his own to get involved with a hunt for whoever sold Gavin's song to Wild World.

"You're supposed to be in L.A. We put you on the bus last night."

"I got off after you left."

"Where'd you sleep?"

"Bus station. I just swapped my ticket for another one in the morning, so it looked like I was just waiting for a bus."

"What about Grandma? She must be worried. . . ."

"I called her last night. Told her I was spending the night at your house, that I'd see her tonight."

Theo frowned. "What's she going to say when she finds out the truth?"

Gavin shrugged. "Can't worry about that right now. I've got to find out who stole my song. That's my future, son—my whole life. You know I'm not good in school like you. And I don't have any real sports talent. I write songs, man. It's what I love and what I want to do for the rest of my life."

Theo felt a twinge of sympathy for his cousin. Earlier that morning, he had checked YouTube, and the video of "Wolfheart" already had over two hundred thousand views. It had gone viral. People from all over the country were commenting on it. Most praised it as the best, most original song they'd heard in a long time. They were calling Wild World geniuses. They thought the band wrote the song. That wasn't right. Theo could understand how that would make Gavin feel.

"Did you contact the band? Wild World?" Theo asked.

"Yeah. All I got was some manager guy who said he didn't know anything about it. I told him I'd sue and he laughed. He said, 'Kid, you know how many times a day you hear that in this business?' And he hung up."

"So, we've got to find whoever took it and get him or her to confess."

Gavin nodded. "That's the only way they'll take my claim seriously."

Theo thought about it. "Who in this school would have the connections to get a song to Wild World? You can't just call them and say you've got a song."

"Where do we start? I'm telling you right now that I don't mind twisting a few arms to get the truth."

"Wait a minute," Theo said. "Why are you suddenly acting so nice to me? Yesterday you called me a thief and a liar."

Gavin chuckled. "Come on, Theo. You know I'm a hothead. I let my mouth run before I've thought things through. Last night at the bus station, my brain had time to catch up to my mouth and I realized you would never do that to me. No matter how much you hate me."

"I don't hate you," Theo said without much conviction.

Gavin bumped shoulders with him. "Theo, man, I know I've given you plenty of cause. I've acted like a jerk to you. I'm not going to get all Dr. Phil or anything. It was what it was. But since I've been writing my songs, I've been seeing things different."

"Like when you tackled me yesterday and tried to choke me to death?"

"Yeah, well, I'm not a hundred percent changed. The old Gavin's still riding shotgun with the new improved version. And sometimes he likes to drive."

"Three words: choke . . . to . . . death."

"I wasn't trying to kill you, cuz, just get your attention."

Theo started walking off. Gavin stayed put. Theo stopped and turned. "Well, let's go. We have a thief to catch. And tell Old Gavin to sit in the backseat."

HAVING Gavin at his school made Theo think of what would happen if you tossed a wild boar into a room six inches deep in farm-fresh eggs.

Squash! Crunch! Splat!

Gavin with Theo's best friend:
Brian approached the lunch table cheerfully, swinging his bulging lunch bag as he walked. The sight of Gavin sitting beside Theo made him freeze in midstep, like someone who sees a cobra curled in the toilet he was about to pee in. The cheerfulness instantly evaporated from his body and he slumped in anticipation of Gavin's insults.

He didn't have to wait long.

"Hey, Chubs, stolen any good songs lately?" Gavin said as a greeting.

"Don't call him that, Gavin," Theo warned.

"What's he doing here?" Brian asked, a slight tremble in his voice.

Theo filled him in. CD missing. Song on Internet. Searching for thief.

"So I'm a suspect?" Brian asked indignantly.

Theo shrugged. "I guess everyone who heard the CD that day is."

"I haven't been suspected of anything since Rabbi Vohen accused me of eating the box of matzo on Passover. Took me an hour and a lot of tears to convince him I was innocent."

"I forgot how much I missed your boring stories, Chubs." Gavin smirked. "Besides, you're not really a suspect. You wouldn't have the guts."

"Oh yeah? Well, I really *did* eat all the matzo. So the joke's on you, Gavin."

Theo laid a hand on his friend's shoulder to calm him.

"How'd you get the school to let him in here?" Brian asked, still huffing with anger.

"I told them the truth. He's my cousin visiting for the day. They gave him a pass."

"Security at this school sucks," Brian said, glaring at Gavin.

Gavin looked around at the buildings and nodded as if impressed. "Pretty fancy setup you boys got here. We find the kid that stole my song, maybe I'll make enough money to go to a place like this. Maybe even this place."

"That removes our incentive to help you," Brian said.

"Whoa, 'incentive.' Did you eat a dictionary?" He patted Brian's stomach. "Or maybe the guy who wrote it."

Brian stepped away from him and slid onto the bench beside Theo. "None of your friends would have taken it," he said to Theo. "It has to be somebody else." He frowned at Gavin. "Maybe one of *your* friends stole it. Or more likely enemies, since I'm sure you have a lot more of those."

"I never played it for nobody!" Gavin barked. "Theo's the only one I let hear my songs." A few kids at other lunch tables looked over.

"Keep it down," Theo cautioned, "or they'll throw you out of here."

"Just for raising my voice?" Gavin laughed. "If they did that at my school, the place would be a ghost town." He took a slice of carrot cake from his tray and slid it across the table toward Brian. "Tell you what, Lyin' Brian. You give me the name of the thief and you can have this big ol' slice of heaven. Yum, yum."

Brian opened his lunch bag and pulled out a bottle of Gatorade, a fat-free yogurt, and celery stalks with peanut butter smeared on them. "Thanks, Gavin. I'm covered."

Gavin laughed. "A diet, huh? I bet you've been on more of those than the number of pimples on your cheeks."

"At least I have the hope of becoming better. You don't."

"Rain give that lunch to you?" Theo asked.

"I'm perfectly capable of making my own lunch, Theo. She just got me started that one time." He took a bite of yogurt. "That reminds me, you heard from Motorpsycho?"

"Who's Motorpsycho?" Gavin asked.

"Some creep who knows Rain," Theo said.

"Who's this Rain chick?" Gavin asked.

Brian and Theo exchanged smiles.

"You'll see," Theo said.

Brian crunched a bite from his peanut butter celery stalk and grinned at Gavin.

Gavin with the Brain Train:

While waiting for Mr. J to arrive, Theo introduced Gavin to the Brain Train team. Everyone but Rain was there.

Upon being introduced, Brooke released a loud snort that said, "I've already forgotten meeting you, chump."

Tunes smiled in his usual friendly way and offered Gavin a fist bump. "What up, dude?"

Gavin did not bump.

"Hey," Daryl said, nodding coolly like he was trying to show he was street tough like Gavin. "Down from L.A., huh? That's cool."

Gavin ignored everyone but Tunes. He pointed his finger at Tunes's face like a gun. "You're the guy that took the CD from Theo's backpack and played my song for everyone."

"That was your song?" Tunes said excitedly. "Man, it is awesome. I saw the Wild World video on YouTube, dude. Have you seen it? Man, they really played the crap out of it."

"Yeah, I saw that, too," Daryl said. "I concur. It's awesome."

"The tune is really catchy. I already know how to play it," Tunes said proudly.

"I especially like your lyrics," Daryl said, and started to sing in a surprisingly good voice:

I think about everything I haven't done.
And everywhere I've never been.
And I howl at the moon.
I just howwwl at the moon.

He howled, and then grinned at Gavin. "Can I get the rest of the lyrics from you, dude?"

Gavin lifted Daryl's backpack from the desk and held it above his head. "Can I beat your face with this, *dude*?"

Daryl winced. "I'd rather you didn't."

"Knock it off, Gavin," Theo said.

Gavin dropped the backpack to the floor and moved in front of Tunes. He grabbed the sides of the desk and leaned forward until his face was just inches from Tunes's frightened one. Tunes leaned back into the chair, but there was nowhere else to go.

"You can play the tune and your pal here knows the lyrics. That seems pretty effing suspicious."

"Dude, it's on the Internet," Tunes said. "Pretty much anyone can play or sing it now."

"That's my point!" Gavin yelled into Tunes's face. "It's *my* song. *Mine!* And now everybody knows it."

"Yeah," Tunes said, "but isn't that kind of the point? Your song is famous."

"But he didn't get paid for it, man," Theo said. "Whoever stole his song and sold it to Wild World is the one profiting from it. And Wild World will profit from it. Everyone but the guy who wrote it."

"That sucks," Tunes said sincerely.

Gavin glared at him. His hands tightened on the desk until his knuckles were white. He started lifting it off the floor. The muscles in his neck and shoulders bulged. It looked as if he was about to toss the whole desk, with Tunes in it, through the window.

"You going for style, or distance?" Rain said as she entered the classroom. "Getting in some practice, in case desk tossing becomes an Olympic event?"

Gavin dropped the desk. Tunes bounced a little at the impact.

Rain lifted the front of the desk Theo was sitting in.

"Hey!" Theo protested.

Rain let go, jolting him. "See? Not that hard to do."

"Oh, brother," Brooke muttered. "Tweedledum and Tweedledumber."

Gavin walked up to Rain, his massive body towering over her like the Hulk over puny Bruce Banner (in those story arcs when they didn't occupy the same body). Theo started to rise. He wasn't sure what he was going to do. He just knew that he wasn't going to let Gavin touch Rain.

It was Rain who touched Gavin.

She poked a finger into his thick chest. "I heard you got ripped off, Song Boy, and now you're stumbling around school like Frankenstein's monster, threatening people. If you really want to find out who did it, you'll need a better plan. Fortunately, I've got one. So shut up and sit down, and let us get on with practice."

Theo couldn't help wincing in anticipation of Gavin's reaction to Rain talking smack to him. But his actual response was not at all what Theo had expected. In fact, it made Theo come to a stunning realization: Gavin wasn't the same guy he was six months ago. The songs showed he had a whole artistic side Theo had never believed in. They also showed that he was in some pain. Sure, he could still be a jerk and a bully at times, but now that seemed less like the real him and more like a role he was playing. An act that he was used to putting on and that everyone expected of him. Theo was confused by this revelation. It made Gavin complicated; Theo almost wished Gavin would go back to simply being a jerk.

The old Gavin might have responded to Rain by setting fire to her backpack or dumping honey in her hair. This Gavin just grinned and said, "You talked the talk, kid. Now you'd better be able to walk the walk."

To which Rain said, "I have no idea what that means, Django. But if you want my help, meet me after school."

To which Gavin said with a smile, "Django. That's good."

To which Mr. J said as he entered the classroom, "Django. Brian, what are they referring to?"

Brian: "*Django Unchained*, the 2012 western movie

about an escaped slave bent on revenge directed by Quentin Tarantino. It's based on a 1966 Italian western starring Franco Nero."

Mr. J: "Excellent. Theo, what does Django have to do with computers?"

Daryl's hand shot up. "Mr. J, should we be discussing an R-rated movie? Isn't that against some sort of school policy?"

"He didn't tell us to watch it, moron," Brooke said.

"True dat," Daryl said, looking around for a smile. "Really? Nothing? I don't care. 'True dat' is coming back."

Mr. J repeated, "Theo, what does Django have to do with computers?"

Theo: "Django is a high-level Python Web framework that encourages rapid development and clean design."

Mr. J: "Very good. Tunes, and Django in music?"

Tunes: "Django Reinhardt, 1910 to 1953, was born Jean Reinhardt. His nickname, 'Django,' is Romanian for 'I awake.' He is considered one of the greatest jazz guitarists of all time."

Mr. J (to Gavin): "And that, young sir, is what we do. If you stay, you play. Otherwise, you may wait outside the classroom."

Theo expected Gavin to glare or scowl or snarl at Mr. J. Instead, his reply couldn't have shocked Theo more if a third arm had shot out of his chest. He said, "Is it okay if I just sit and listen? I'll be quiet."

Mr. J nodded and gestured toward a seat at the back of

the class. Gavin went to the desk and sat quietly for the rest of the practice.

Afterward, they agreed to meet up with Brian and Rain after school to figure out who the thief was. Once the mystery was solved, Theo assumed Gavin would tie him into a tiny pretzel and shove him into a greasy Dumpster. Just for old times' sake.

For now, Theo had his own problems. Like staying on the team. Make that *teams*.

Gavin with the basketball team:
With Gavin watching from the bleachers, Theo found himself trying even harder. Not that he wanted to impress his cousin, he just . . . Okay, he did want to impress him.

"Lob it in to Theo," Coach called from the sidelines. They were running the same drill for the two-millionth time.

Chris Richards passed the ball to Theo.

Theo caught it, spun toward the basket, and ran into the Great China Wall (a.k.a. Roger McDonald). Theo's teeth rattled and cartoon birds spun around his head.

"Traveling," Sinjin said.

The impact had caused Theo to shuffle his pivot foot.

Roger smirked.

Coach came over, trying hard not to look exasperated. "The move was good, Theo, but you have to anticipate your guy will be there. Where else would he be? So, like we talked about before, fake the spin to the right, then spin to the left. Get him to move. That way if he bumps you, it's a foul. Got it?"

"Got it, Coach," Theo said.

"Okay. Again."

They ran the play again. Theo caught the ball, spun to the right as the fake, then spun to the left. This time Sinjin swatted the ball from his hands, snagged it on the fly, and dribbled away.

Theo looked over at Gavin, expecting to see a smug grin. But he didn't look sneering and superior. He didn't look embarrassed. He just watched with no expression.

"Keep the ball up, Theo," Coach called. "Out of their reach. Use your height. What's the point of being tall if you don't use it? Run it again."

They ran the play a few more times. When Roger and Sinjin double-teamed him, Theo tossed the ball out to unguarded Chris, who sank a ten-footer.

"Yes!" Coach hollered. "Yesyesyes!"

But the very next play, Theo tried to do the same thing and Sami Russell darted in to intercept the pass.

"You've got to mix it up, Theo," Coach said. "Don't be predictable."

And so on.

Finally, it was over. When everyone headed for the locker room, Gavin merged with the players and fell into step with Theo.

"I think what the coach meant," Gavin said, "is you need to spin with a little more power." Suddenly he whirled around as if to demonstrate, "accidentally" crashing into Roger. The impact sent Roger toppling backward, his hand flailing out for balance. His flailing hand smacked Sinjin in the face.

"Oh, sorry, guys," Gavin said. "My bad." He looked at Theo and smirked.

Theo might have smirked, too.

GAVIN, Theo, and Rain climbed down out of the municipal bus and started walking toward the tall office building.

"He's in here?" Gavin asked Rain.

"Yup," she replied.

The front of the building was old-fashioned red brick for about fifteen feet up. Then the brick stopped with a zigzag edge that resembled a broken eggshell. From inside the brick facing, a black steel-and-glass building rose thirty stories high, as if hatched from that brick egg. This was the Henderson Building.

Theo looked up, shading his eyes. "Looks like something out of a sci-fi movie. Where the bad guys make their evil plans to release a supervirus—"

"That turns poor people into mindless slaves," Rain interrupted.

"But first they need to use their secret time machine—"

"To go back in time to get the missing ingredient to make the virus work—"

"Uh, uh, uh . . ." Theo faltered, thinking. Then: "The tears of a child. Because in the future, everyone is too numb to cry."

"Yes!" Rain exclaimed. "That's good."

Theo smiled proudly.

"If you two are finished nerd-flirting," Gavin said with a growl, "let's get this done."

"We weren't flirting," Theo said, heat rising to his cheeks in embarrassment.

Rain laughed. "Boys," she said, shaking her head. "I'll go in and check the place out. Three kids wandering around might look like a few rabid fans seeking autographs or something."

Gavin nodded and Rain disappeared into the building.

Theo and Gavin waited in silence.

By the time they'd met up with Rain after school, she'd already done some research on the Internet and made a few calls. She had a plan of action, and since Gavin's only plan had been to scowl and threaten students until someone confessed, they agreed her plan was better.

And here they were.

After a few minutes, Gavin said, "She's cool."

Theo shrugged as if he had no opinion.

Gavin grinned. "Listen, little cuz, this isn't the time to play it all frosty gangsta. She's smart, you're smart. She's cute, you look like the backside of a dog. Match made in geek heaven."

Theo shrugged again. "Yeah, well . . ." He didn't know what to say. He'd never talked about anything personal with Gavin before. It felt like some sort of trap.

"That Brain Train thing you do," Gavin continued.

Here it comes, thought Theo. I knew it was a trap. Now he'll make some typical cruel remark about a bunch of dweebs who know useless info that only our parents can appreciate. Which is good, because we'll be living in their basements for the rest of our lives.

Instead, he said, "I get it, Theo. You guys pushing each other to be smarter. Like you're all survivors in some jungle, sharpening your brains like spears, so you can go out into the world to hunt. Kinda like the way I'm always trying to get better at writing songs. It was pretty cool to watch."

Theo just stared at his cousin. This couldn't be the same Gavin who yanked Theo's jeans down in front of everyone at last year's Thanksgiving dinner and hollered, "Who wants a turkey leg?"

"And since I'm in a Yoda mood," Gavin said, "here's what I noticed about you playing basketball at practice today."

Theo inhaled as if getting ready to take a punch to the stomach. Gavin couldn't have anything positive to say about that practice.

"It seems to me," Gavin said, "that you play like you're ashamed of being tall. Like it's a curse rather than an advantage. You play like you're apologizing for your height. You know what I mean?"

"No."

Gavin sighed. "It's like you think you're some kind of freak and they're doing you a favor letting you play. Like I told you before, you can't play like you're afraid to lose. You gotta play like you know you're gonna win."

Theo started to protest, but then said, "What about you? Why are you so bold in everything but your music? Why not share it?"

Gavin looked down. "I share it," he said in a low voice. "With my mom. She's heard everything. It's kind of like a special link between us. I don't know how to explain it."

"What does she say about your music?"

"She's my mom, bro—what's she gonna say, except it's the best thing since Mozart." He laughed. "She keeps telling me I should share it, too. But I'd rather get punched in the face than play it for somebody else."

"Then why'd you play it for me?"

Gavin didn't say anything for a minute. Then he grinned and said, "Because you remind me of my mom, all girlie and stuff." He punched Theo playfully, clearly trying to change the subject.

Before Theo could say anything, the door to the building opened and Rain waved for them to follow her.

Ten minutes later and twenty-one stories higher, they entered a reception area through huge glass doors. The space was as large as a classroom. The floor and walls were marble, except for one wall, which was a black waterfall. The receptionist sat behind a marble and wood counter. Behind her on the wall were large gold letters spelling out MOONSILVER, KRAMER, DOBSON, AND SCHWARTZ—ATTORNEYS-AT-LAW.

Rain spoke to the receptionist, a chubby guy in a shiny black suit and bright red bow tie who looked like the Nordstrom's shoe salesmen who used to wait on Theo's mom. At first, he seemed to be trying to get rid of Rain. But he had underestimated her. She just kept talking, her hand gestures getting more animated as she spoke. Finally, he made a phone call and relayed whatever she had told him.

Three minutes later, a young woman in a tight beige skirt and silky blue blouse escorted them down a long hall of offices. Behind each etched-glass door a worker was hunched over his or her computer keyboard, or writing furiously on a yellow legal pad, or both. The place was so busy with well-dressed men and women that it seemed like this suite of offices was somehow responsible for everything important that was going on in the world. Just thinking about it made Theo's stomach tighten with anxiety.

"Almost there," Blue Blouse said pleasantly. Every step of her high heels clacked against the marble floor like gunshots in a video game.

When they arrived at the right door, Blue Blouse held it open for them to enter.

"Ms. Moonsilver?" Blue Blouse said. "The children are here."

"Children?" Gavin snapped. "We're not ch—"

Rain laid a calming hand on Gavin's arm. He stopped speaking, though clearly he was still agitated.

They entered the office. It was three times as big as any of the others they'd passed. One wall was floor-to-ceiling glass, with a sweeping view of much of Orange County. From twenty-one stories up, Theo could see two different freeways, South Coast Plaza shopping mall, a community college, and far into the hazy distance, a sliver of the Pacific Ocean. The view gave him the feeling that the window was a windshield and the person who sat in this office steered the entire county from here.

Behind the giant desk sat a middle-aged woman with midnight-black hair that had a gray streak on either side, like parentheses around her face. She wore turquoise-and-silver earrings and bracelets. She also had a silky blouse, but hers was the kind of white you'd only see somewhere in the Arctic where no one has ever touched the snow.

Her desk was so massive it probably could be seen from outer space.

Theo, Rain, and Gavin sat down across from her in equally massive red leather chairs. The chair made Theo feel like he should be commanding a starship.

"So nice of you to see us without an appointment, Ms. Moonsilver," Rain said politely to the woman.

Moonsilver? The name finally registered for Theo. It was one of the names in gold on the lobby wall. She was one of the owners of this law firm.

Ms. Moonsilver didn't smile or offer to shake hands.

Instead, she picked up a gold clock from her desk and turned it around so they could see it.

"You said you had important information about a crime committed by our clients Wild World. You have exactly five minutes to convince me this isn't some kind of childish prank. After that, I'll have security escort you from the building. Whether it's into a waiting police car is entirely up to you."

"You're Native American," Gavin said.

"Indian," she corrected. "We call ourselves Indians. We let the rest of the world worry about being politically correct." She tapped the clock. "You now have four minutes left."

Gavin stood up and snatched the clock into his fist as if he were about to throw it against the wall. "Your clients are thieves, and I'm going to sue them! I don't care how many fancy lawyers they have."

Ms. Moonsilver showed no emotion. Neither fear, nor anger, nor even interest.

Rain said calmly, "Sit down, Gavin."

He replaced the clock and plopped back down in the chair, staring at Ms. Moonsilver.

Rain explained everything.

Ms. Moonsilver listened, again without any emotion. When Rain finished, she stood up. "Wait here," she said, and left the room.

They sat in silence, staring out of the huge window.

Ms. Moonsilver returned and walked briskly back to

her desk. She sat down and looked at Rain, Gavin, and Theo with a stern frown. "I've checked the appropriate documents, and here's the situation: Someone approached my clients with the song 'Wolfheart.' My clients agreed to purchase it. The seller already had the proper contracts and release forms with them, including a statement of ownership. The agreed-upon payment was made. So, as far as my clients are concerned, they acted in good faith and are not liable in any way. If you have a claim, it would be against the seller."

"Who is the seller?" Gavin demanded.

"I'm afraid I can't give you that information. Client confidentiality. Which means I can't legally discuss in any more detail my clients' business. Which also means that we're done here. You may leave."

The three of them were stunned. Even Rain.

"That's it?" Gavin said, jumping to his feet. "We come all the way down here and that's all you tell us?"

"I didn't ask you to come here," Ms. Moonsilver said.

"One more question," Rain said. "How did you get the song to go viral so quickly?"

Ms. Moonsilver almost smiled. "You can't make anything go viral. All you can do is send it to all the popular sites and bloggers. If they like it, they'll pass it on. And if others like, they'll pass it on. In the end, the video or song still has to have something special. This song has that something."

"Yeah, I know," Gavin said. "I wrote it."

"Not in the eyes of the law. You'll have to prove it in a courtroom."

An hour later they were all sitting on a picnic table at Palisades Park. They'd been quiet on the bus. Defeated.

"Well," Gavin said to Rain, "any more brilliant plans?"

"I'm thinking," she said.

After a couple more minutes of silence, they heard a motorcycle roaring nearby. They looked over by the restroom/snack building. Motorpsycho sat on the bike, revving his engine. He flipped open his helmet and stared at them.

"Who's this clown?" Gavin asked.

"Motorpsycho," Theo said.

Gavin stood up. "I'm just in the right mood to meet him."

Rain stood up, too. "No. I'll talk to him."

"He hit you last time," Theo reminded her.

"He won't do that again," Rain said. Theo didn't know how she could be sure of that.

Theo started to get up, tripped, and fell against Rain. She caught him and kept him from falling.

"Smooth, bro," Gavin said.

Theo straightened himself up and said to Rain, "Sorry."

"Just don't do that on the basketball court," she said. She walked off to talk to Motorpsycho.

Theo and Gavin watched.

Rain and Motorpsycho spoke heatedly. Theo couldn't

hear the exact words, but he could hear the tone, which was angry.

Suddenly Motorpsycho handed her a spare helmet. She put it on and climbed onto the back of his motorcycle.

"Wait!" Theo shouted, springing to his feet and running toward them.

They rode off.

"TURN right at the stop sign," Theo called, pointing at the street ahead.

Gavin pedaled through the stop sign as he swung the bike right down Gardenia Street with Theo close behind. It wasn't like Theo to ignore traffic rules, but they were on a rescue mission. Maybe. Plus, the residential streets were empty right now. Except for the occasional jogger mom pushing a special jogging stroller.

"Pull over!" Theo shouted at Gavin. They both braked at the curb while Theo studied the map on Gavin's phone screen.

Here's what had happened back at the park: When Theo saw that Rain was going to go talk to Motorpsycho, he'd pretended to stumble into her. What he was actually doing was slipping his iPhone into her backpack. Once the motorcycle had roared away, he'd used Gavin's phone to activate the GPS finder that allowed them to track his own phone. Then they went back to Theo's house, grabbed his and his dad's bikes, and pedaled off to find Rain and discover her secret connection with Motorpsycho.

"How close are we?" Gavin asked.

Theo was a little pleased to see that, while he was breathing normally, Gavin was breathing hard. Theo's basketball conditioning had finally paid off. "Just a few more blocks," he said, tapping the screen to enlarge the map.

They took off, side by side at first, then with Gavin lagging slightly behind. Finally, they pulled up in front of a two-story white house with a couple of motorcycles and a black Lexus in the driveway. There was a small yard, and a flower-filled garden surrounded the house.

The house looked normal, just like Theo's and Brian's and Daryl's and Tunes's. There was a tricycle in the driveway, so there had to be a little kid. What kind of evil could they be doing inside with a tricycle outside?

Theo's heart was pounding. Now what? He didn't really have a plan.

Gavin had taken out a cigarette and was about to light it when Theo ran over to him and blew out the lighter flame. "Put that away! No wonder you were wheezing from that bike ride."

Gavin shrugged and put the cigarette back in the pack.

Theo took a deep breath and marched up to the front door. He knocked briskly. Gavin walked up and stood behind him. "Don't worry, cuz. I've got your back."

But Theo was worried. This was someone's home. Private property. What right did he have to snoop into whatever was happening inside?

The door opened. Motorpsycho stood glaring at Theo.

"What are you doing here?" he growled.

"I, uh . . ." Theo stuttered. Gavin started to push his way around Theo to take over, but Theo blocked him and said, "Where's Rain? We want to talk to her."

"What you want means nothing to me. Now go. You are not welcome here."

"Hey, man," Gavin said angrily, trying to push his way around Theo again. Theo used his basketball skills to box him out.

"We just want to talk to Rain first," Theo said. "Then we'll go."

Motorpsycho took a menacing step toward Theo, but Theo didn't back down.

Suddenly Rain appeared at the doorway and shoved Motorpsycho aside. She said something harsh to him in a foreign language. Then to Theo, "What are you doing here?"

"I wanted—"

"*We* wanted," Gavin corrected.

"We wanted to make sure you were okay."

Motorcycle snorted and said something in the foreign language to which Rain responded.

"Matar," a man called from inside, "show your friends in. It's not polite to keep them waiting."

"Yes, Uncle," Rain said.

"Matar?" Theo said.

Rain shrugged. "Well, come in, then. You're just in time."

"In time for what?" Theo asked as he and Gavin stepped inside the house.

"For the trial," Rain said.

Motorpsycho slammed the door behind them and locked it.

"AS-SALAMU *alaykum,*" the man said with a big, friendly smile. He gestured for Theo and Gavin to have a seat on the white sofa.

Theo and Gavin just stood and stared.

The man speaking was tall and dark-skinned (though not as dark as Theo). He wore a suit and tie. His mustache and beard were as black as his hair.

"That's Arabic," Rain said. "It means 'peace be unto you.' In case it ever comes up in the Aca-lympics." She smiled as if to put Theo at ease.

Theo was not put at ease.

Standing next to the bearded man was a woman whose head was wrapped in a bright yellow scarf so that no hair was visible. She wore a long, flowing, blue robe. Sitting on the stairs was an older teen girl. She wore jeans and a UCLA sweatshirt, but she also had a green scarf covering her hair. She was texting on her phone and didn't look up at Theo or Gavin.

Across the room stood Motorpsycho and another guy, in his early twenties. He wore a leather bomber jacket that

Theo recognized from the park. He was the other motorcyclist who had been with Motorpsycho. Shadow Man.

A little boy of about seven ran into the room carrying a light saber. He looked around and then ran up the stairs, jostling the girl who was texting. She muttered, "Jerk," without missing a peck on the keyboard.

"Don't run on the stairs, Mamun," the older woman cautioned.

Mamun instantly stopped and walked up the rest of the flight, but when he got to the top, they heard his footsteps running down the hall as he shouted, "Run, you Klingon scum!"

Everyone (except Text Girl on the stairs) was staring at Theo. He didn't know what to say, so he blurted, "Mamun's mixing up his movies. Light sabers are from *Star Wars*; Klingons are from *Star Trek*." Like a true geek, when in doubt, he fell back on facts.

"You're Muslims," Gavin said as if accusing them of being chicken thieves.

Motorpsycho and Shadow Man sneered. If the rest of the family had noticed Gavin's tone, they didn't show it. They all smiled pleasantly as if they were entertaining long-lost relatives.

"Yes, indeed, we are Muslims," the man said. "My name is Razeem Hamid. This is my wife, Fadilah. And my daughter, Ni'ja, who had better put her phone away if she wishes to keep it."

Ni'ja/Text Girl immediately slipped her phone into her

back pocket with an accompanying eye roll and sigh.

"And you've met three of my sons. Mamun the Jedi, and . . ."—he pointed to Motorpsycho and Shadow Man—"Aadil and Aazim."

Theo didn't look at them. He focused on the man and woman. "I'm Theo. This is my cousin, Gavin." Theo shook the hands of the mother and father. Gavin just nodded.

Theo said, "I don't understand. Rain said this was some sort of trial. If it is, I'd just like to speak on her behalf."

The man, his wife, and Text Girl laughed.

"I'm not on trial," Rain said. She pointed at Motorpsycho and Shadow Man. "They are."

"'Trial' is too harsh a word, Matar," the mother said to Rain.

"Matar?" Gavin said.

The mother smiled. "Matar means 'rain' in Arabic. It is a blessed name. We come from a dry desert area, so rain is always a blessing."

"It's pretty," Theo said.

Rain made a face at Theo.

"Yes, it is," the mother said. "It is Muslim tradition to choose a name with a righteous meaning that will benefit the child throughout their life. However, she prefers the English word. Just as she prefers the American way of dressing."

"So do I," Ni'ja said. "Why can't I go by Nancy? Then I wouldn't have all the boys calling me Ninja."

The mother said, "Ni'ja means 'saved one.' What does Nancy mean?"

"It means 'talks to boys,'" she said sarcastically.

"Actually," Theo said, "Nancy is of Hebrew origin, from the name Ann, meaning 'grace.'"

Razeem smiled at Theo. "You are a very smart young man, Theo. Rain has chosen her friends well."

Rain rolled her eyes. "Uncle Razeem, you sound like some Arab villain in a movie. Relax. Theo's just a nerd, and Gavin is a songwriter who probably thinks all Muslims are wearing suicide bombs while shopping for groceries."

Motorpsycho said something to Shadow Man in what Theo now realized was Arabic. They smirked.

"Aadil! Aazim!" their father snapped. "It is rude not to speak English in front of our guests."

Both boys glared at Theo and Gavin, but they stopped talking.

Rain grabbed Theo and Gavin by the upper arms and pulled them toward the front door. "Uncle, I'm going to let you guys get on with your nontrial or whatever while I explain everything to my friends."

"Can I go with them?" Text Girl asked hopefully.

The mother shot her a stern look and Ni'ja sighed with defeat.

"Nice meeting you," Theo said to the family (though he didn't look at the brothers).

When the door closed, Rain dug into her pocket and

pulled out Theo's iPhone. She handed it to him.

"When did you find it?" Theo asked.

Rain laughed. "As soon as you stuck it in. You're not exactly James Bond."

Theo looked puzzled. "Then why didn't you say something?"

"She wanted you to follow her, dipstick," Gavin said.

Rain said, "I just wanted you to make the effort. To care enough to take the risk."

Theo scoffed. "Why can't girls just say what they mean? Why all this mumbo jumbo?"

"I *am* saying what I mean, Theo," Rain said. "You're just not listening. It's like your basketball game. You play like all you care about is what other people think of you, not because you care about the game. That keeps you from really being in the game."

"I'm 'in' the game," Theo said. "Believe me, I'm way in the game."

She threw up her hands in frustration. "Okay, let's look at it another way. When you were pedaling over here to save me, what did you feel?"

"Winded," Gavin said.

"Not you," Rain said.

Theo thought, but he couldn't come up with anything. "I don't know. Why do you always have to be feeling something? Maybe I wasn't feeling anything."

"Weren't you worried about what your cousin would think? Going through all this trouble and effort for a girl?

Especially a girl you hardly know who's done nothing but keep secrets from you?"

Theo was surprised to realize he hadn't thought about that. Normally that would have been his first concern. He would have been afraid of Gavin making fun of him.

Rain continued, "Weren't you scared that when you found me you'd have to deal with my cousins?"

"Yeah, I was, but I just . . ." Theo let the sentence trail off, because he wasn't sure how to finish it. On some level he'd been afraid, but that level had been buried under ten tons of something else. "Look, don't make this a big deal. I just thought you were in trouble, and I didn't want anything bad to happen to you. I would have done the same for a stranger."

Rain raised a skeptical eyebrow.

"Not everything is a big life lesson, you know. Some things just happen." It's what Theo used to say to his mom.

Rain smiled. "Anyway, thanks. Both of you."

"Except you weren't really in trouble," Gavin said, an edge to his voice. "You were hanging with a bunch of Muslims. Does that mean you're a Muslim?"

"Yes," Rain said.

"But you don't wear one of those scarves," Theo said.

"A *hijab*," Rain explained. "It's not required by the Qur'an. We're only supposed to dress modestly. What that means is open to interpretation. Some believe it means wearing only a scarf, others believe it means covering everything but the eyes. Some even cover the eyes with a mesh veil. I believe I already dress modestly."

Gavin started walking toward the bikes. "She's fine, man. Let's get going. We still have a thief to catch."

Theo didn't move. He said to Rain, "I still don't understand what's going on with you. Why did your cousin hit you that day in the park? Why was he threatening me?"

Rain sat on the stoop. Theo sat beside her.

Gavin kicked impatiently at a clod of dirt.

"My mom's a Muslim from Iraq, and my dad's a Quaker from Pennsylvania. He's a contractor who met my mom while he was in Iraq rebuilding an airport. She wanted me to be raised Muslim, and so I'm Muslim. Whether I'll stay one for my entire life, I don't know. I'm still figuring things out. But right now I am."

"Where are your parents?"

"They had to go back to Iraq. My grandfather died, and they have to see about bringing my grandmother over here. So they left me with my mom's brother, Uncle Razeem."

"And he's very strict?" Theo asked, guessing at why she'd been so keen to leave.

Rain laughed. "No, he's a very sweet man. And Auntie Fadilah is like a mother to me. But their sons, Aadil and Aazim." She shook her head distastefully. "In the past year they've become more and more religiously conservative. They think it's their right to tell me how to behave, because I'm a girl. What I should wear. How I should behave. Who I could talk to."

"My mom was raised Baptist," Theo said. "I've seen the same thing in some of those families."

"Sometimes they search my bedroom and backpack, looking for evidence that I'm not behaving properly. They even cut up one of my Dr. J shirts, because they think girls shouldn't play basketball. When I got tired of their bullying, I left and stayed at a friend's house for a few nights. I didn't want them to get into trouble, so I told my aunt and uncle that I was working on a school project with my friend and this would be more convenient. But after a couple days, Auntie Fadilah figured it out. That's why the family meeting inside."

"The trial," Theo said.

"Basically."

"Why didn't Ni'ja complain? And why don't her brothers go all conservative on her, too?"

"She's nineteen and goes to UCLA. They think she's too far gone. I'm only thirteen, so they think they can still force me into their idea of a Muslim."

Theo noticed her T-shirt for the first time. The single lowercase word: HOWEVER.

"What's going to happen to your cousins?" Theo asked.

"Who cares?" Gavin said with annoyance. "She's fine. They're screwed. Happy ending. Let's go."

Theo ignored him.

"Aadil, who you call Motorpsycho, will probably lose his motorcycle for a month. His sister will have to drive him to school and work. That should be humiliation enough for him."

Theo smiled.

"As for Aazim, he's older and lives on his own, so Uncle Razeem's influence isn't as strong. However, he works for Uncle's close friend at a Toyota dealership, so I foresee some late shifts and lots of dirty work there."

Theo looked Rain in the eyes. "Why didn't you just tell me when you first met me?"

"Because . . ." Rain sighed. "Because everyone at my old school knew I was Muslim, and I had to put up with so much terrorist talk that I couldn't take it anymore. We were near the Marine base, so we got a lot of kids from military families. A couple weeks ago, I convinced my auntie and uncle to let me transfer."

"That's why I hadn't seen you around school before," Theo said.

"They didn't want me to transfer. They said it was giving in to bullies and that running away never solved anything. They were right, of course. I knew that even then. But I ran anyway."

"So you were kind of the Sasquatch of your old school," Theo teased.

"Not because of my height, obviously. But yeah, you could say I stood out in the crowd." Rain smiled. "That's why I gravitated to you, I guess. We have some things in common. Except I'm a much better basketball player."

"We'll see," Theo said with a grin. Suddenly he snapped his fingers. "Hey, that's why you picked the pepperonis off Brian's pizza that day at lunch. You're kosher, or whatever the Muslim version of kosher is."

"Halal," Rain said, "which means 'lawful.' And, yes, we don't eat pork."

"Brian's Jewish, but that doesn't stop him."

Rain shrugged. "I've been known to sample bacon on occasion."

Gavin, unable to contain himself any longer, marched over to them. "I've got two words for you, cuz: Nine. Eleven. Get it? Here's two more words: al-Qaeda. These folks got jihad on the brain, man. They want to bomb us all into being Muslims."

Theo winced. So much for his thinking that Gavin had changed for the better. . . . He looked at Rain to see how she would react to the harsh words.

Rain burst into laughter. "Boy, that stuff never gets old. It's good to stick with the classics." To Theo: "Now you see what I was up against at school. Try listening to that every single day. And the threats." She turned to Gavin. "Okay, Gavin. Here's a cheat-sheet guide to Islamic beliefs. First, we believe there's only one God, the same one Christians and Jews believe in. Second, we believe in the Scriptures, which include the Old and New Testaments and the Qur'an. Third, we believe there's a day when we'll all be judged and our souls will go either to Paradise or Hellfire.

To be honest, I'm not so sure about that one, but I'll hang with it for a while longer. How is that so different from most people you know?"

Gavin ignored her question and said, "Then why are so many Muslims violent? They got a jihad against us."

"A jihad is when someone struggles to have good conquer evil. When you find a lost wallet with a hundred bucks in it, you struggle over whether to keep the money or return it. That's jihad. All the violence is a few evil people using religion to get other stuff they want. The rest of us are just trying to figure out how to do the right thing."

Gavin didn't say anything.

"Look," Rain said, "I'm not hoping for a G-rated ending here where everybody holds hands and sings about world peace."

"Then what are you hoping for?" Gavin said.

"Kindness," Rain said. "Isn't that what you would hope for if you were a minority?"

"Very funny," Gavin said, grabbing one of the bicycles. "Stay here if you want, Theo. I have better things to do," he said, and then rode off.

Theo watched Gavin leave. But he was thinking about something else. He was thinking about all the kids he knew who had broken families like his. Not unhappy, just broken, like a chunk had been torn away. A dead mother. A runaway father. A mother in Africa. Parents in Iraq. Not like the ideal families you see in a lot of TV shows. Most just trying to do the best they could. Like Rain said, people just want to do the right thing. And parents, especially, want to do the right thing for their children.

"Theo?" Rain said after a while. "You okay?"

"Huh?" Theo refocused on her and smiled broadly. "I think I just figured out who the thief is."

"Who?" Rain said excitedly.

Theo quickly climbed onto his bike. "Tomorrow," he said as he started pedaling away.

"HOLY crap!" Theo's dad said as he entered the kitchen. He looked as surprised as Theo had ever seen him before.

It was Thursday morning. Tomorrow might be Black Friday, the day that ended Theo's run on the Brain Train and the basketball team, but today was going to be his. Today he would reveal the thief who stole Gavin's song and sold it to Wild World. At least he would have this one victory to call his own.

"What's going on here, Theo?" his father asked, more stunned than angry.

"What do you mean?" Theo said innocently as he poured more pancake batter into the black skillet. "I'm just making breakfast."

"For how *many*?"

What Marcus meant was: Theo already had several plates stacked high with pancakes, a huge bowl brimming over with scrambled eggs, a serving plate piled three inches high with fried bacon, and a large pile of paper plates, plastic forks, plastic cups, and napkins on the kitchen table. Three pitchers of orange juice stood next to the plastic cups.

"Seriously, Theo," Marcus said with some concern, "are you okay? Are you having headaches or thoughts of hurting yourself? You're not experimenting on neighborhood pets, are you?"

"Define 'experimenting,'" Theo said.

Marcus just stared.

Theo laughed. "I'm fine, Dad. Everything's under control. Sit down and help yourself."

Marcus sat at the table, took a paper plate, and scooped out some scrambled eggs. The whole time he stared at Theo as if this was a horror film and he expected his son to suddenly skitter up the wall like an insect.

"I've been thinking, Dad," Theo said, flipping a pancake in the skillet. "You should go out on a date. Like with a girl."

Marcus paused in midbite. "Is that what this super-breakfast is about?"

"No. I'll explain that in a moment." Theo pointed his spatula at Marcus. "It's time someone else had to put up with you. I can't be expected to laugh at your lame jokes all by myself. That's child cruelty."

"Oh, really? And what brought on this new Cupid attitude?"

Theo took a deep breath. It was time to tell the truth. Sort of. "I know about your online dating, Dad."

Marcus laid his fork down on the table. Theo could see the cop part of his dad figuring everything out: Theo sneaking into his computer, cracking the password, reading his personal file. But the dad part of him chose not to mention it right now. Theo really appreciated the dad part.

"I don't know," Marcus said quietly. He looked guilty, like an art thief with a long rap sheet who'd been caught with the blueprints to a museum. "Seems like it would complicate things. Our life."

Theo considered that. Their life together was pretty good. But then he thought about what his dad did after Theo went to bed. Did he watch the same TV shows he used to watch with Mom? Did he laugh at something funny and turn to see if she was laughing, too, only to be reminded that he was alone? How long should he have to live that way?

"You know what I think?" Theo asked. "I think our lives get complicated all on their own, without any help from us. So, if we have a chance to complicate it in some way that we want, I say we should go for it. As someone told me recently, you have to make the effort, take the risk."

They ate in silence for a few minutes. His dad reached for a pancake and said, "It's one thing to grow tall, it's another to grow up. I think you've managed both pretty nicely."

The doorbell rang.

As Theo hurried off to answer it, he muttered under his breath, "I hope you still feel that way after breakfast."

Theo returned to the kitchen with Miranda Sanjume behind him. She was dressed in a dark blue, pin-striped pants suit. She looked very professional.

Marcus jumped to his feet. "Miranda? What are you doing here?"

Miranda looked surprised. "Didn't you send me a text message asking me to come right over?"

"That was me," Theo said. "I used his phone."

"Theo!" his dad snapped. "What are you—"

The doorbell rang again.

"Hold that murderous thought," Theo said, rushing off to answer the door.

When he returned, the basketball team was with him.

"Not much seating, guys," Theo said, "so you'll have to stand while you eat. Go ahead, dig in."

"Hey, Mr. Rollins," Chris Richards said. The rest of the team followed with greetings, which Marcus returned.

"Where's Coach?" Roger demanded, looking around. "And why did he want to have a team meeting here?"

"He didn't," Theo explained cheerfully. "I sent those texts and e-mails. It's not that hard to create a ghost account that mimics someone else."

"Not very hard," Miranda said, "but very illegal."

"You're an attorney, right?" Theo asked.

Miranda turned to Theo's dad. "Marcus, what's this about?"

"Wait a minute!" Roger said. "So Coach didn't call this meeting?"

"Correct," Theo said.

Roger looked around for the rest of the team to join his outrage, but they were busy grabbing food.

The doorbell rang.

"For the love of . . ." Marcus said, exasperated. "Theo, what is going on here?"

"Soon, Dad," Theo said, running off.

When he returned, he had the Brain Train with him: Brian, Tunes, Daryl, and even Brooke.

"What are they doing here?" Brian asked, looking at the basketball team.

Brooke snorted. "Better question is, what are *we* doing here?"

"I thought Mr. J called a meeting here," Daryl said in confusion.

"Obviously, Theo faked it," Brooke said. She smirked at Theo. "Which means when Mr. J finds out, he'll kick you off the team for sure."

"We'll see," Theo said.

"Theo!" Marcus growled. "Answers! Now!"

Doorbell.

"Manners first, Dad." Theo exited and returned with Rain.

"Rain," Theo said, "this is my dad. And that's Miranda Sanjume, attorney-at-law."

"Hi," Rain said. To Theo: "What are you up to? Your lawn looks like a bicycle shop."

The kitchen was packed to the point of people bumping

shoulders as they heaped food onto their plates.

"Hey, hey! Save some for me!" Gavin hollered as he strolled into the kitchen.

"Gavin?" Marcus said. "Where did you come from?"

"Theo's room," Gavin said with a yawn. "He hid me there last night."

Marcus jumped to his feet. "Does your grandmother know where you are?"

Gavin pointed to Theo. "This is his show, Uncle Marcus. He's the man with the plan."

Theo patted his dad's shoulder as he slipped by. "All taken care of, Dad. She knows he's here with us."

"But *why* is he here with us?" Marcus asked. "In fact, why are all these other people here with us? Why did you turn our home into a cafeteria?"

Tom Farley, the team's best free throw shooter, spoke around a mouth full of pancake. "I can't be late for school, dude."

"'Denouement'!" Brian said excitedly. "Right, Theo?"

"Denoue-what?" Roger said.

"Denouement," Brian repeated. "It's the part at the end of a mystery when the detective reveals the killer." To Rain: "It was one of the words we had to define at last year's Aca-lympics."

Everyone fell silent and stared at Theo. Even his dad.

Theo said, "Yes, that's why we're here. I invited everyone who's suspected of stealing Gavin's song 'Wolfheart,' and then secretly selling it to Wild World."

"That's your song?" Weston Zheng said. "I saw the video. It's cool."

Gavin didn't say anything, but Theo could tell he was pleased.

"Wait," Roger said. "I was a suspect?"

"Me, too?" Sinjin James protested.

Theo held up his hands as if quieting a crowd. "The point is, I figured out who the real thief is."

"Who?" Brian asked.

"Who cares?" Brooke said with a bored roll of the eyes. "I'm leaving."

"It's Brooke, right?" Tunes said. "The killer always tries to leave first."

"Oh, for goodness' sake," Brooke said. "Just finish this up already." She stood, arms crossed, glaring at Theo.

"It had to be someone with access to the CD," Theo said. "Which is everyone in this room. I had it at the Brain Train practice and at basketball practice. The two most likely places for it to be stolen."

Marcus interrupted, "Theo, maybe this isn't the best time for this."

"No, Dad," Theo said. "It's the perfect time. They want to know what happened, right?"

Most muttered agreement. Others just kept stuffing pancakes into their mouths.

"The other thing the thief needed was access," Theo said. "Access to the music industry so they could make this deal happen abnormally fast."

Everyone started to look at one another suspiciously, trying to figure out by the way they chewed bacon or drank orange juice which one had connections to the music industry.

"Tunes plays piano concerts," Roger accused. "He must know people."

Gavin pushed through the others to confront Tunes. "You little—"

"It wasn't me!" Tunes said in a panic. "I don't know anybody. My piano teacher arranges my concerts. I just show up and play."

"It's not Tunes," Theo said. Then he looked straight at his dad. "Right, Dad?"

All eyes swiveled onto Marcus.

He sighed.

Gavin's mouth dropped open. "Uncle Marcus?"

"He didn't do it alone." Theo nodded at Miranda. "I saw your profile on the dating site. Those photos of you with front-row seats at all those rock concerts."

"Theo!" Marcus said.

"You can punish me later for using your computer, Dad. Right now this is about the truth. The truth is, you contacted Miranda, not to date her, but because she's an entertainment attorney, specializing in the music industry."

Gavin's face was red with anger. "You stole my song and sold it?"

Theo hurriedly continued: "He didn't steal it, Gavin.

Not really. I was thinking about something Rain said yesterday about people wanting to do the right thing. And that made me think about all the kids from homes with divorced or dead or absentee parents."

A few of the kids in the kitchen nodded in recognition. Even Gavin.

"And I was thinking about how those parents all still try to do the right thing by their kids. And how hard it is to know what the right thing is sometimes. But you've still got to make the effort. Take the risk that it is the right thing."

Rain smiled at him. "Copycat."

Gavin jumped in angrily. "How is stealing my song the 'right thing'?"

Theo's father stood up. "I didn't steal it, Gavin," he said. "After listening to it, I realized just how really talented you are. I Skyped your mom in Africa and told her that we should do something with it. Something to get you past your fear of sharing your work."

Gavin started to protest, but stopped. It was true, after all.

"She agreed. But I didn't know what to do. I remembered seeing Miranda's profile, saw the photos, and reached the same conclusion Theo did."

"You could have just looked entertainment attorneys up online," Brooke said.

Marcus grinned. "Okay, maybe the song wasn't my only reason to call her."

Miranda grinned, too.

Brooke made a gagging sound. "Ewwww."

"Anyway," Marcus continued, "Miranda knew Wild World's attorney—"

"Karen Moonsilver," Miranda said. "She went to law school with my dad. I e-mailed the song to her, she e-mailed it to Wild World's agent, and he gave it Wild World. They loved it, drew up a contract—"

"Which I didn't sign," Gavin said.

"But your mother did, electronically. You're a minor, so your signature isn't really required here. All the money we got for the song and any future royalties will be deposited in a bank account in your name."

"How much did you get?" Gavin asked.

Everyone grew quiet, waiting to hear the amount.

Miranda smiled, leaned into Gavin's ear, and whispered.

Gavin's eyes widened. *"What?"* he asked, as if he didn't think he'd heard it right.

She whispered again.

Gavin looked up at his uncle. "Whoa."

Marcus added, "We couldn't tell you earlier because the bonus clause in your contract doesn't kick in until the video has reached half a million views. Which it already has, and then some."

"Bonus clause?" Gavin said.

"Means you get more money," Miranda said.

"And you will have complete control over all your other songs," Marcus said. "This was a onetime deal. Just a little kick start. After this, it's up to you and your mom to make all the decisions."

Chris Richards looked at his watch. "Well, this has been interesting, but now it's time for me to get going. Congratulations, Gavin," he said sincerely, and left. The rest of the team followed. Several also congratulated Gavin. Roger and Sinjin didn't.

Brooke left without saying anything. Through the window, Theo watched her climb into an SUV waiting at the curb. No bicycle for her.

The Brain Train also departed. On the way out, Tunes insisted that Gavin take him to watch Wild World record his next song.

"See you at school, dude," Brian said to Theo with a big smile. "Best breakfast ever. So theatrical."

"The new me," Theo said. "Taking risks."

Brian held up his sack lunch of healthy foods. "Me, too."

Rain, wearing a T-shirt with the word INEVITABLE on it, squeezed Theo's hand. "They say 'go big or go home.' Now, this is what I call Going Big." She left.

Miranda also took off, saying she was late for work. Just before she stepped out of the house, she looked at Marcus and mouthed, "Call me."

He smiled back and nodded.

When everyone was gone, Theo, Gavin, and Marcus just sat there in silence, letting everything settle into their minds.

Finally, Marcus looked around the disastrous mess that was the kitchen and said, "Guess who's cleaning this up."

Gavin got up and headed for Theo's room. "Not me. I didn't tell him to make breakfast."

"And I've got to go to work," Marcus said. He stood up, went to the safe to retrieve his gun, and yelled good-bye as he hurried to the garage.

Theo looked around at the dirty pans, spilled food, filthy counters, and bacon-soaked paper towels. He hadn't expected to be carried off on everyone's shoulders, but he hadn't expected this either.

Tomorrow was Friday. The day of his showdowns with the Brain Train and the basketball team. Uncovering the thief hadn't changed anything in his life.

But then: "Let's get to it, cuz," Gavin said, walking over to the table and gathering up the used cups and plates. "This place won't clean itself."

"I have school," Theo said.

"No problem. I can handle it. Least I can do."

"Thanks." Theo started for the door. He usually walked to school, because it gave him time to think, but if he rode his bike, he'd almost be on time. He opened the front door, looked back into the kitchen. Gavin was hunched over the sink, scrubbing the skillet. He was about to tell Gavin not to use soap, just water, and rub a little cooking oil in it afterward. Like his dad taught him.

Instead, he dropped his backpack on the floor and went

back to the kitchen. Without a word, he began cleaning the counters. Gavin didn't look at him, but Theo could see the smile on his cousin's face.

When they were done, Theo called his dad and asked if he could stay home. Because Theo hadn't missed any days so far this semester, Marcus agreed to call the school and let them know Theo would be absent today.

"What about Brain Train practice? And basketball practice?" Gavin said. "Tomorrow's the big day."

"I'll study the Aca-lympic manual this morning, and in the afternoon I'll kick your butt in one-on-one at the park."

Gavin laughed. "Man, you've really let this Sherlock Holmes crap go to your head. Fortunately, I'm here to give you a reality check."

Theo was true to his word. He studied in the morning, then worked on his basketball moves with Gavin. This behavior wasn't like the old Theo, but he had come to realize that, given the things he'd done lately, he'd grown out of that Theo the way a snake grows out of its old skin, sheds it, and leaves it behind forever.

The "new Theo" came to some decisions about what he would do tomorrow that surprised even him.

WAS that really Mr. J standing in front of the Brain Train? Theo wondered.

His hair was cut even shorter, heavily gelled, and combed straight back like a porcupine. He wore a black suit, yellow shirt, and red tie as shiny as an ironed eel. No one at the school wore a suit or tie, not even the teachers or administrators. This was California, dude.

"We missed you at practice yesterday," Mr. J said to Theo.

"Sorry," Theo said. He didn't mention anything about being sick or make any other excuses. He was tired of lying.

"No worries. I assume you used some of the time to study the manual in preparation for today?"

"I did," Theo said truthfully.

"Excellent." Mr. J rubbed his hands together like he was about to eat something delicious. "Shall we get on with the showdown? Constance versus Theo in the Crackdown in the Classroom! Get reaaady to rummmmmble."

Constance squirmed nervously in her seat. She glanced

at Brooke, who grinned triumphantly at Theo.

Daryl raised his hand. "Mr. J, did you have a stroke or something?"

Everyone laughed. Except Brooke.

"Why do you ask, Daryl?" Mr. J said.

"Your hair. Your clothes. Your . . . you."

Mr. J looked surprised. "You don't like my new hippie clothes?"

"Those aren't hippie clothes, Mr. J. Hippies don't wear ties and suits."

"So, I'm not a hippie now? What am I, then?"

Daryl shrugged. "To tell you the truth, we've been asking ourselves that question for a couple years now."

Everyone laughed again. Except Brooke.

"You look a little like a mobster," Daryl said. "Like in *The Godfather*."

"No," Brian disagreed. "More like a heavy-hitter businessman in *Wall Street*."

"Leo in *The Aviator*," Tunes said.

They threw around a few other movies before Mr. J held up his hands to silence them.

"I'm sure you'll eventually figure out what movie I belong in. But for now, we have a showdown to get to. A Battle of the Brains. Combat of the Craniums. War of the Wits . . ."

He might have gone on like that much longer (he had an unusual love of alliteration), but Theo stood up, interrupting him. "Mr. J?"

"Yes, Theo?"

"I've decided to concede my position on the Brain Train to Constance. I think she deserves it for her dedication and knowledge. She will be a great asset to the team. If it's okay, I'll take her place on the alternate team until I prove myself worthy again."

Mr. J looked out at the rest of the team.

Only Constance and Brooke showed any surprise.

"This is some kind of trick, Mr. J," Brooke said. She looked at Theo suspiciously, as if she thought he might have water balloons stashed under his shirt.

"How does this trick work, Brooke?" Mr. J asked. "What does Theo gain?"

Brooke's face reddened as she tried to figure out Theo's brilliant plan.

"Anyone else want to comment?" Mr. J asked, looking around at the others.

No one spoke. Theo had already informed Tunes and Daryl of his decision before the meeting. He'd told Brian last night. They'd all tried to talk him out of it, but Theo had made them understand that he was doing the right thing. At least he thought it was the right thing, and that's all he could hope for.

"Nothing?" Mr. J asked. He turned and smiled at Theo as if he'd been expecting Theo to do this all along. "Well, well," he said. "Remember, Theo, 'No sensible decision can be made any longer without taking into account not only the world as it is, but the world as it will be.'"

Theo stood up, thanked everyone, told Mr. J he'd be at the practice for the alternates, and started out of the room. Just before he exited through the door, he said to Mr. J, "That quote is from science-fiction writer Isaac Asimov."

And then he left.

"THERE'S an actual crowd out there!" Weston announced as the team dressed for their game.

"What do you mean by 'crowd'?" Roger said. "Like six people instead of the usual three?"

Sinjin laughed and they bumped fists.

"More like fifty." Weston pointed at Theo. "Your pals from the Brain Whatever are there."

Theo hurriedly tied his Nikes and ran over to the locker-room door. He opened it a crack and peeked out. Brian, Daryl, Tunes, and Constance were sitting with Mr. J. No Brooke, of course. Brian made a goofy face for Constance and she laughed. Go, Brian, Theo thought.

He was about to close the door when he saw Rain climbing the bleachers. With her were her aunt, uncle, and cousin Text Girl. Ni'ja looked appropriately bored and inconvenienced, but she marched up the bleachers as her parents directed her. As soon as she sat down, she whipped out her phone and began stabbing the screen with her finger.

On the bottom bleacher, right behind the team table, in his crisp blue uniform, sat Theo's dad. Beside him in her pin-striped suit sat attorney-at-law Miranda Sanjume. She whispered in Marcus's ear and he laughed.

Seeing his dad laugh made Theo smile.

"Heard you quit the Brain Strain," Chris Richards said. He'd walked up behind Theo so silently that Theo jumped when he heard the words.

"Brain Train," Theo corrected as his heart thumped crazily in his chest.

"I know. I'm just messing with you."

Theo grinned. He'd never heard Chris crack a joke before. "Actually, I didn't quit. Just dropped down to the alternate squad."

"What happens if you get kicked off the basketball team? Can you get your old position back?"

"I don't know. I don't think I'd try. Wouldn't be fair to Constance. She's the girl who took my place."

Chris nodded solemnly. "Guess you'd better keep your place on this team, then, huh?" Then he walked away.

Theo ran as hard as he could after Number 5, a.k.a. Gorilla in a Jersey. If Theo was long and gangly like a giraffe, this kid was as thick and powerful as a gorilla. Worse, he was also fast. He was four feet in front of Theo when his feet hit the paint. His long arms stretched up as he called for the ball: "Open! Open!"

Gorilla's teammate saw him in the open and threw a long pass from half-court. Gorilla easily snagged the ball and made a layup just before Theo finally caught up to him.

Score: Lemon Hill 8, Orangetree 4.

As Coach had warned, the Lemon Hill boys were bigger than Theo's team. Theo was still the tallest player on the court, but almost every other player from Lemon Hill was taller than everyone on the Orangetree team. Most of them looked like they had mustaches coming in and even some chin whiskers. Theo wouldn't have been surprised to learn that they all had arrived here on motorcycles.

Their coach, a former Brigham Young center, was taller than Theo. He'd taught his team how to use their size, and that's exactly what they were doing. Nothing deliberately rough, just good body placement.

That's what Gorilla was doing now to Theo.

Theo backed toward the basket, one arm outstretched for the ball. Just as he had done in practice. But Gorilla planted his powerful body behind him, and no matter how much Theo tried to push back or slide around, Gorilla held his ground.

Sami lobbed the ball to Theo. Theo, unable to get closer to the basket, passed it to Chris.

Theo wrestled for a better position and called for the ball again.

Chris passed the ball in to Theo.

Theo deliberately dribbled more than he ordinarily would, in the hopes of drawing Chris's defender to double-team him.

Chris's defender took the bait and lunged to steal the ball from Theo.

The rest of the plan was for Theo to toss the ball to the unguarded Chris, who would shoot the ten-footer.

But suddenly Chris's defender slapped the ball away in Theo's mid-dribble, and Lemon Tree grabbed the loose ball and charged up the court to their basket.

Score: Lemon Hill 13, Orangetree 8.

Theo sat on the bench, toweling the sweat from his face.

He was starting to dread that today's game was going to be just like every other practice and pickup game he'd ever played. With him looking like a fool and causing his team to lose. What had he been thinking? He'd quit Brain Train (okay, dropped to the alternate) in order to focus his attention on basketball. He figured that not having Brain Train as a backup would make him give his all to this game. Unfortunately, his all was crap.

"Get ready, Theo," Coach said. "You're going in."

Theo sighed. *Really, Coach? Haven't you figured out yet that this plan isn't working?* But he said nothing, just waited for the next whistle for him to go back in.

"Hey, Sasquatch!"

Theo turned, looked up into the bleachers.

Rain waved. "Use those ginormous feet to kick some butt!"

Theo smiled. At least he could still smile, despite a tsunami of humiliation.

The whistle blew and Theo went in for Thomas Farley. They slapped hands as they passed.

Gorilla was waiting for him with a grin. He gestured for Theo to stand beside him.

Then from the stands, Theo heard Rain start chanting, "Sasquatch! Sasquatch! Sasquatch!"

Theo's dad and Miranda joined in: "Sasquatch! Sasquatch! Sasquatch!"

Others took up the chant: "Sasquatch! Sasquatch! Sasquatch!"

Theo didn't know what to do with that. Sure, it was flattering, but it also heaped a couple hundred tons of extra pressure on his shoulders.

After Roger missed a desperate three-pointer, Lemon Hill easily grabbed the rebound.

Gorilla broke free and sprinted for his basket. This looked like it was going to be the same play as before, with Theo running as hard as he could but still trailing behind by four feet. He had to do something else.

He looked over his shoulder and saw Chris swarming Number 8, who had the ball. Chris put such pressure on him that he stopped dribbling. Now he had to pass. Roger, Weston, and Sinjin were doing a good job of blocking their guys, so they couldn't receive the pass.

The point of being tall is to use it, Gavin had said. But that didn't mean Theo had to stop using his brains. He didn't have to rely *only* on being tall. Basketball was a lot like chess—pieces with different skills moving around a confined space. You just had to play it on the run, the way Mr. J had taught them.

Theo looked over the basketball court and imagined it as a chessboard. Suddenly he had a crazy idea. He deliberately slowed down, letting Gorilla widen the gap between them. With enough distance between him and Theo, Gorilla also slowed down. Theo turned and saw that Number 8 was in trouble.

"Chris!" Theo called.

Chris quick-glanced at Theo, and then at Gorilla.

Everything depended on Chris understanding what Theo was doing.

Chris did. He eased his defense, giving Number 8 the chance for a long pass down the sideline. Gorilla saw this and cut for the sideline. Number 8 threw the ball in a high arc.

Just as Theo had planned.

Theo dashed for the sideline. True, Gorilla was faster. True, Gorilla was closer to the hoop. Once he caught the ball, he'd be able to jog in for an easy, unopposed layup.

But as the ball started to drop out of its arc, Theo,

in full run, leaped as high as he could. His long arms stretched up, up, up. He intercepted the pass, landed, fired the ball to Chris. Chris bounce-passed to Roger, and then set a pick on Roger's defender. Just as Roger slid to the side behind the pick, Chris rolled off and ran straight to the hoop. Roger threw the ball to Chris, and Chris laid it in for two points.

The crowd on the Orangetree bleachers hollered and stomped their feet.

Theo saw his dad cheering and clapping.

Rain had her hands cupped around her mouth and was shouting something that got lost in the general cheering. But from her expression, Theo knew it was something good.

Score: Lemon Hill 22, Orangetree 20.

Theo was in the paint again.

Gorilla was blocking him out. Again.

Theo was too far away for a layup. He lowered his body and tried to nudge Gorilla backward. No go.

This was the exact position they'd been in the last time, when Lemon Hill had stolen the ball from Theo.

Theo raised his hand for the ball and Weston lobbed it in. Unable to get a good shot, Theo dribbled to draw off Chris's defender. The defender, remembering his last success, took a couple steps toward Theo in an effort to steal the ball.

Theo immediately rocketed a pass to Chris. But Chris's

defender was tall and quick. He was instantly in Chris's face, making a shot impossible.

They're chess pieces on a board, Theo thought. Don't just use your height to play, use it to fool them.

Theo raised his hand again. "Chris! Chris!" There was more urgency and confidence in his voice than ever before. He knew exactly what to do.

Chris looked at Theo, seemed to recognize the change in his voice, and lobbed it over his defender into Theo's hands.

Theo stared at Chris and gestured with his head what he wanted Chris to do. Theo wasn't sure if Chris understood, but he hoped so. Otherwise, this was going to be a major fail.

Theo went through the usual motions, dribbling and backing in, though there was no actual backing in against Gorilla. Suddenly he spun around, as if to toss up a hook shot. All the players looked up as Theo's huge hand soared above them.

There was no ball there.

He'd tucked it in the crook of his left arm.

Chris grabbed the ball from there as he ran around Theo's left side. Like an expert purse snatcher on the run.

Theo came out of his fake hook and slid to the left. Chris's defender slammed into Theo's back, sending Theo face forward into Gorilla's granite back. Theo flopped down to the ground in a daze.

As he fell, he turned enough to see Chris toss in an easy bank shot.

Score: Lemon Hill 26, Orangetree 26.

In the movies, games like this are always tied and come down to a final shot with two seconds on the clock. In the movies, Theo would take that shot. In the movies, it would go in and they'd win.

That's not what happened here.

Despite Orangetree's best efforts and the enthusiastic cheering from the crowd, Lemon Hill won by a comfortable margin: 38–30.

During the remainder of the game, Theo had tried a few more innovative plays with his team. Some worked. Some didn't.

Yet again no one hoisted Theo onto their shoulders and carried him around in triumph. Roger and Sinjin didn't come up after the game to beg forgiveness for the horrible way they'd treated him. Chris didn't high-five him and promise that they'd be best friends the rest of the season.

Instead, Coach said, "Good game," to all of them, talked about how awesome they'd all played, and finished with, "See you all at practice on Monday."

And that was that.

But to Theo, it was the happiest day of his life.

TWO weeks later:

"Have you ever actually touched a basketball before?" Theo asked. He had suggested basketball as part of Brian's weight-loss plan.

Brian bounced the ball awkwardly in front of him. First with one hand, then with both hands. "Let me think," he said. "Gerry Turner threw one at my head in third grade, remember? Technically that means my forehead touched a basketball, so my answer is yes."

They were standing on the court at Palisades Park. Most of the courts were empty, because it was too early for the pickup games. Theo was teaching Brian how to shoot. Brian hurled the ball at the basket as if it was a rotten melon he was trying to get rid of. The ball hit the bottom of the net, then bounced onto the grass.

"Nothing but net!" Brian said triumphantly. Theo smiled.

It had been an eventful two weeks since the Lemon Hill game.

Theo had taken his place with the alternates on the Brain Train, helping the first team prepare for next week's match against Lansing. He was glad to have some of the pressure off of him while he pursued basketball.

In the Ravens' next game, against Turtle Rock Middle School, Theo had been so "in" the game that he was actually surprised when the final buzzer sounded. He was also surprised by his performance: he'd scored six points, assisted on eight others, and blocked three shots that caused turnovers. They'd won, and Coach took them all out after the game to celebrate. Over pizza they clinked root-beer mugs to toast Chris Richards, who had scored a career high of eighteen points. Roger had passed a basket of onion rings to Theo without sneering or saying something sarcastic, so there was hope even there.

Gavin had taken Theo and Rain to watch Wild World record one of Gavin's songs at a studio. Wild World had signed demo CDs for Rain and Theo.

Theo's dad had started dating Miranda. They were making plans to drive to L.A. for a concert of some Motown tribute band that Theo had never heard of. The three of them had eaten out together a couple times. Once, Miranda complained about how a judge had treated her, and Theo and his dad made her put a dollar in the BIB jar. She'd laughed as she'd stuffed the money in, which was a good sign.

Theo's dad had changed his computer password.

"Uh-oh," Brian said, tossing the basketball to Theo. "Here comes the ol' ball 'n chain."

Theo looked over and saw Rain jogging across the park toward them.

"Really?" Theo said to Brian. "Ball 'n chain? You're going with that?"

"Whatever, dude. Dieting saps my originality."

"How much weight have you lost?"

"Four pounds. But they were four of the heavier pounds."

Theo laughed.

Rain ran up to them, her cheeks red from exertion. She smelled like gingerbread. Theo liked gingerbread.

She reached into her pocket and pulled out a granola bar. She handed it to Brian, who quickly peeled the cellophane wrapper like it was a banana.

While chewing, he said, "You don't have to feed me every time you see me, you know. I already have a mother."

"You want me to stop?"

"Of course not. A Jewish boy can never have too many mothers."

Rain laughed and pulled off her orange hoodie, dropping it on the ground. Underneath she wore a white T-shirt with the word FINALLY in small black letters on the chest. She grabbed the ball from Brian's hands and dribbled out onto the court. "You boys ready to play?"

Theo looked at the word *finally* on her shirt and smiled.

For the first time he knew exactly what she meant without having to puzzle over it. Kind of like shooting a basketball and knowing it is going to go in the net before it even leaves your fingers. Some things you just know.

"I'm ready," he said, running onto the court.